Something's Cooking at Dove Acres

A New/Young Adult Novel
by Will Zeilinger
Copyright 2011

Copyright © 2011
by Will Zeilinger

All rights reserved except as permitted under the U.S. Copyright Act of 1976, no pert of this publication may be reproduced, distributed, or transmitted in any form or by any means, or stored in a database or retrieval system without prior written permission of the publisher.
Shorebird Publishers
Janet Elizabeth Lynn and Will Zeilinger
Post Office Box 91073
Long Beach, CA 90809-1073

The characters and events portrayed in this book are fictitious. Any similarity to real persons, living or dead, is coincidental and not intended by the author.
Thank you for respecting the hard work of this author.

First Edition: April 2011

ISBN-13: 978-1-9863-9595-3
ISBN-10: 1986395952
Ebook ISBN: 978-1-4661-3188-0

Cover design by Those Designers

Printed in the United States of America

To my wife and love of my life, Janet
for all her help and inspiration
And to all the young people in my life for
reminding me that being young is only temporary

Other Novels by
Will Zeilinger
www.willzeilingerauthor.com

- The Naked Groom
- The Final Checkpoint

Skylar Drake Mystery Series
by
Will Zeilinger
and
Janet Elizabeth Lynn

- Slivers of Glass
- Strange Markings
- Desert Ice
- Slick Deal

Chapter One

I wanted to kill Luke Garrett more than I hated washing dishes, but my mother told me I'd be on my own someday. What I didn't know was it would be the summer I graduated from high school. Yuck, I really needed a dishwasher, a cute one with blue eyes... or maybe a regular one that fits under the counter.

Did I hear the doorbell? Whenever I turn on the water I think I hear the phone or doorbell. I shut off the water and listened... it actually was the doorbell.

I leaned out the window and looked toward the front door. "Hey, Jojo!" I yelled. She backed up, squinted at me and pulled off her floppy hat. She was dressed in cargo shorts, and hiking boots.

"Madeline Van der Wald! It IS you. I heard a rumor that you were on the island."

I wiped my hands and ran to the door. Killing Luke Garrett would have to wait until after I talked to my best friend. I threw open the door and gave her a giant hug.

"What on earth are you doing here, Jojo?" Even though I hadn't seen her in two years, I missed her.

"Me? I'm working over at Smuggler's Cove. They finally promoted me from Aide to Camp Counselor. But why are you living out here on the island alone?"

"I'm stuck here for at least six months, maybe more."

JoJo smiled and shrieked, "six months? That is so cool! We'll be out here together this summer. Wait... are you, like a house sitter?"

"Well, no. Actually, I own it."

"What? So you're like rich now? How did that happen? Everyone knows Dove Acres is the biggest private estate on Catalina Island!"

"Actually, WE own it. My mother's Aunt Helen left it to her, but since she and Dad died in that car accident, it went to me - well, us actually."

"You mean I was in the will too?"

"No, but since they took you in, I think it's only fair."

"Wow." Jojo responded, "I-I don't know what to say."

I held her hand, "Do you have to go or can you hang for a while?"

"Sure, I don't have to go back to camp until the new crop of kids arrives in a couple days. That's why I stopped to check out the rumor that you were up here. By the way - what are all the holes I saw driving in? They look new? Are you planting trees already?"

"No. I don't know where those came from. I've only been here two days. I'll ask my aunt's lawyer when I see him tomorrow.

I took her hand and led her to the kitchen.

"Maddie, how come I never even heard of this Aunt Helen? Was she like really old?"

"Well yeah, but that's not why she died. She was watching a demo of some humongus, do-everything, propane barbeque grill at the convention center when the thing blew up. Barbequed weiners went flying everywhere and a piece of the metal bun warmer hit her in the head, killing her instantly. At least that's the story her lawyer told me.

I pulled a couple stools out from the breakfast bar, "Want some lemonade?"

She smiled and nodded.

"Just out of curiosity," I asked, "have you ever heard of a guy out here named Luke Garrett?"

She practically choked on an ice cube when she heard his name.

"Luke Garrett? His father, Mr. Charles Garrett II owns the moving company, the trash company, and has something to do with Island Conservation. Yeah, I'm familiar with the name. Why?"

I've known Jojo long enough to tell when she was lying - pretending she didn't know him. So I played along.

"He works for his father's companies." She swirled the lemonade in her glass. "Why, have you met him?"

"Not exactly, he tried to kill me two days ago."

Jojo put her glass down and fiddled with the tiny gold key on the chain around her neck. "What? Who? Luke? What are you talking about?"

"I just stepped off the boat and he tried to run over me with a big green garbage truck. That is... if this is the same guy." Jojo listened intently as I continued, "He's about six feet tall, really cut, about twenty, twenty-two... maybe older..."

"Steel gray eyes, a tight, skinny butt and totally hot." She finished my sentence for me. When she discovered what she'd said, her eyes widened and she gulped down some more lemonade.

"That sounds like the same guy."

She cleared her throat, "It could be him. Yeah it sounds like Luke." With a little cough she asked, "Tell me what happened."

Something was going on. I wasn't sure. Maybe she went out with him or else she's stalking him. With his looks, I was surprised he wasn't being followed around by every female on the island.

"Okay, so I was at the boat dock trying to load my bags into my little rented golf cart when he comes speeding down the road towards me in that giant truck. I had to literally jump out of the way and landed on my tush in the gutter. Then, check this out, he stopped and yelled at ME like it was my fault that he didn't know how to drive! There was a big rip in my new silk skirt and I had blood on my hand from where I scraped my thigh on the curb, see?" I pulled up one side of my shorts and showed her my road rash.

"So he yells, 'What are you doing in the middle of the road anyway? You better stay on the sidewalk unless you wanna get squashed. This isn't Disneyland.' I mean, shit Jojo - Who the Hell did he think he was? So he put his hand out like he wanted to help me up, but I just waved him off. This guy was lucky I didn't kick him."

Jojo took another gulp, "Then what?"

"He just shrugged and said, 'Suit yourself.' I saw his shirt and it said, *Catalina Disposal* on one pocket and *Luke Garrett* on the other."

"Well," Jojo responded, "that wasn't a very nice welcome to Avalon."

"Can you believe this guy? When he walked away, I stuck my tongue out at him, I mean what's with, 'This isn't Disneyland'? What a jerk."

"Listen," Jojo asked as she held her empty glass out to me, "don't you have anything stronger than lemonade? Maybe a beer, at least?"

I shook my head.

"Sorry, I haven't found anything in the house yet. I get the feeling my aunt didn't drink much."

"So you've been here a whole two days? Who brought you up here?"

"It's just been me doing the whole thing." I picked up a big envelope off the counter. "See this? It came by courier before I came over here with all the keys and stuff in it. It must weigh two pounds." I shook it to jingle the keys when an index card fell out with "Safe Key in box" typed on it.

Jojo picked it up, "What's this? Safe key? There's a safe?"

"Don't know, I saw that card yesterday." I turned the envelope out onto the table. "Where's the key? There's no box either."

We ran up the stairs to my room and zipped opened my wheeled carry-on. "If it's in a box, it must have fallen out of the envelope on the trip, but I don't remember seeing it anywhere."

Together we checked the bedroom. Jojo looked under the bed while I checked my carry-on again.

"If there's a safe, maybe it's hidden behind a painting or mirror like in a movie." So we walked through the house checking behind every painting, photograph and mirror on the walls, joking that maybe the safe was stuffed with jewelry and cash. I was starting to get pangs of guilt for feeling so greedy.

"Nothing," Jojo said when she flopped on the living room sofa. "Maybe it's in a closet. How many rooms are there?"

"Let me think... Seven bedrooms, a parlor, den, library, dining room, kitchen and three bathrooms, plus a laundry room and the garage."

Jojo looked up at me, "It could be anywhere. Maybe it's not even here."

"Come on." I took her hand, "Get up, let me show you something."

Jojo followed me upstairs to a bedroom where I had been sifting through some boxes full of photographs and junk.

"I started going through all this stuff last night and threw out a whole pile already. Now, what am I supposed to do with the rest of this? There's just so much."

Jojo crossed her arms and stood back. "Okay, I have an idea." She lined up the boxes along the edge of the bed and turned each one on end. From her pocket she pulled a thick marker pen.

"Do you always carry one of those around?"

She shrugged, "I use it for making little signs at camp." Jojo pulled off the cap. "Now we're gonna label each of these boxes." She picked one up, "Like this one, for instance." Very neatly she printed "Photos" on the side. "We'll label the next one important looking papers, then jewelry, knick-knacks, coins, and so on. Oh, and one for odd bits."

I flipped through a stack of photos my Aunt Helen had taken at our home in Santa Ana. One was shot at Christmas some years ago. My aunt was posing by the fireplace in a long black velvet skirt and burgundy sweater pinned with a large brooch. I think I remember that dress.

"Aren't you scared being up here alone - in the middle of nowhere?" Jojo asked. "I'm not trying to scare you, I was just asking."

I set the photos on my lap and stared at her. "Why did you say that? I didn't even think about being scared until now. Last night I heard weird noises, but I figured it was the wind or this old house or maybe some kind of critters outside, y'know, like possums or raccoons."

Jojo gave me a hug, "I'm sorry, that was mean."

I turned the photograph over and read; *I'm wearing great grandmama's platinum/diamond brooch from Tiffany's New York. Van der Wald's House – Xmas 1990*, written in pencil on the back.

"Diamonds and platinum? Tiffany's?" I shouted, "Oh shit!"

"Was that a good or bad oh shit?"

Jojo grabbed the photo and rubbed her finger over the brooch. "Platinum? I've never touched anything made of Platinum."

I paced back and forth with my hand on my forehead, "It looked too big and clunky to be real... Y'know? Like fake costume Jewelry."

"Where is it?"

"Shit Jojo, I tossed it in a trash bag and took it to the garage with all the other trash bags full of junk."

"So," Jojo replied, "I guess it's bad." She examined the photograph carefully and announced. "Okay, new rule. You are not allowed to toss anything else until we check out all the stuff in the garage."

"What other valuable stuff did you toss out? I remember back in High School everyone thought you were the übershopper." Jojo said, "You knew what everything was worth."

I wiped my eyes and took her downstairs through the kitchen to the garage.

"Maybe all the stories are true after all and there is a fortune hidden up here."

I glanced back at her, "What stories?"

"Oh, just kids at the camp gossiping about buried Indian treasure, Mafia money or pirate gold. It depends on who's telling the story... Wait. You mean you've never heard any of this stuff?"

"Come on Jojo, I'm just looking for a pin I might have thrown out, not a sunken Spanish galleon. Those are just kids making up stories about things that are none of their business just to impress the other kids."

Jojo shrugged, "Hey I'm just telling you what I've heard."

I flipped on the lights and hit the garage opener button. "Oh shit, shit, shit! The garbage bags I put out last night are gone. The trash must have been picked up this morning."

"Maddie, didn't you hear the trash truck? It's so quiet up here."

"I was wiped out. Okay I was little scared about being up here alone. I had some warm milk and toast to help me relax. I must have slept right through it."

Just then we saw a Catalina Disposal Truck lumbering up the drive. JoJo waved it over toward the garage. It swung around in a cloud of dust and backed up to the door.

It was Luke Garrett. The same jerk that almost ran over me.

"Hey Jojo!" Luke yelled over the noise of the diesel truck and hopped down off the seat. Bright red lipstick was smeared on his mouth and across one cheek. I guessed he was with someone who didn't want him to leave.

Drop-jawed, Jojo stared at him but I pretended to ignore it.

He reached into the cab and shut off the engine so he wouldn't have to shout over it while I pointed to my checkbook and yelled, "DO I PAY YOU NOW OR WILL YOU BILL ME?" He looked over his shoulder at me and shook his head until the engine noise stopped which I took to mean pay him later, so I stuffed the checkbook back in my pocket.

Luke pulled off his gloves, "Just wanted to pick up the next load of trash on my way back to the plant." He squinted into the empty garage, "You mean you don't have more trash? Didn't you say in your voice message that you needed two pickups today or are you still mad about your skirt? I'll have my father pay to have it repaired."

JoJo stepped close to him and flicked his collar with her finger, "You better look in the mirror - Now." She whispered.

Luke leaned back to look in one of his big, square fender mirrors and blushed, "Dammit Raylene," and tried to rub it off with the back of his hand. "Sorry about that." He shrugged, "Long story... complicated."

"Listen Luke," I crossed my arms, "Something very important was accidentally thrown in the trash that you already picked up this morning." He waited silently while looking right at me.

"... and well," I continued, "I need to get it back."

"Oh, sure," He pulled the truck door open, "Come by the plant later this afternoon and you can go through the bags." JoJo looked at him, then me, "We gotta go. See ya later." She poked me in the back with her knuckle and pushed me into the garage.

As the door came down, Luke shouted under the door, "And Maddie, y'better wear something you can get dirty!" The door clunked shut, leaving Luke standing alone in the dusty driveway wiping the rest of the lipstick off his face.

She pushed me through the door to the kitchen, "Ow, why'd you do that?" where she peeked through the curtains and watched him drive away. "What's with the attitude Maddie?" She asked, "They are the ONLY trash company on the island and we need him."

I jerked the curtains shut, "Did you see the way he showed up here?"

"Why should you care about that Maddie? You just got here and don't even know him."

"Is he married?" I felt really stupid asking that.

"No, I'm pretty sure he's not married. But I'm not so sure about the girlfriend thing, except for Raylene at Pinkie's Market."

"Tell me about this Raylene who is she?"

"She's just this very young, very cute blonde that works at the market in the summer and... she has a major crush on Luke. But then a lot of the women on the island think he's hot."

"Well," I shrugged, "Showing up like he just rolled out of her bed wasn't very professional. I don't know why it bothered me so much."

Jojo gathered up her backpack and hat. I went to the door with her and gave her another hug. She plopped her hat on her head and said, "Think about it Maddie... you'll figure it out."

Chapter Two

My aunt's lawyer was supposed to be here at eleven-thirty and it was almost one. I was thinking that he could have at least called when I saw a four-seater golf cart came putting up the road. Out stepped a man wearing a suit and carrying a big square briefcase. Nobody I've met on the island dressed like that.

"Well hello Maddie Vander-Girl," He smiled a big, tooth-whitened, fake-looking grin. "Tom Silverman." He put is hand out. "Remember me?"

I did have a fuzzy memory of someone calling me that when I was a kid, but it couldn't have been him. Maybe it was his father.

We shook hands and I showed him to the dining room.

He opened the briefcase and dropped a stack of file folders on the table. "How's everything going? You all settled into this magnificent place?"

"I'm okay."

"Well," he flipped open the case, "I'll try to keep this simple and not use to much financial mumbo-jumbo."

"Whatever. I mean, that's fine I guess."

He patted the palm of his hand on the stack of papers and looked me in the eye, "I have good and bad news, you can decide which you want to hear first."

"I really don't care. I had to go through something like this when my parents were killed. Let's start with good news."

"Okay, fine - ahem, then we'll get right to the terms of the inheritance... Well, here, you read it." He pushed the folder towards me.

I opened it expecting to read pages and pages of "legalese" stuff that I wouldn't understand, but instead I read:

1. Stay on the island for six consecutive months.
2. Maintain the property (Dove Acres) as always.
3. Present the check (enclosed) to Javier

I stopped reading, "This is it? Just this list." I looked for more pages. "That should be easy, and then Dove Acres is mine, free and clear?

Tom sat back and nodded. "That's all you have to do."

"Who is this Javier?" I asked.

"He cares for the horses and was one of Helen's long time friends. He lives here on the island."

"We have horses?"

He looked at me for a minute, "You mean you haven't seen the stables? Have you seen the whole estate?"

"Not really. This morning is my third day and I've been busy getting settled, cleaning the dust off stuff. I knew I heard horses."

"When we finish signing a few things we can go for a ride and see the property."

I really felt stupid, but I continued reading the list aloud,

"4. Maintain livestock,"

"5. If I am unable or unwilling to abide by the terms of this agreement then Lloyd Brewster will assume the inheritance and all things pertaining thereto."

I closed the folder. "Who is Lloyd Brewster?"

"He is your third cousin, once removed, currently residing in Purgatory Springs, Missouri."

"Oh. Well, this is all pretty clear. I don't see a problem with anything here."

"Okay then," He rubbed his hands together and flipped open another file folder. "now for the bad news. Your aunt wasn't a person who understood money. When your Uncle George died, your aunt didn't even know how to balance her bank statement.

I tried several times to explain it to her and so did their accountant, but she never got it." He flipped through several more files and papers, "So it appears you are presently secure, financially that is... but only on paper. Your inheritance, unfortunately, is a disaster. There were back taxes, property taxes and several other debts she had accrued...,"

He lost me after property taxes.

"As a result," Tom continued, "when things started to look bad, she refused to acknowledge it. She wanted to maintain her extravagant lifestyle which consisted of travel and throwing elaborate parties. Last year her accountant threw up his hands and quit. It's a shame too, he was a good guy."

"So those parties cost a bundle, right? I've seen the photos."

"Let me show you something Maddie. I want you to see the rest of the estate before I go any further."

We drove along the bumpy road in his rented cart until a large barn appeared just past a grove of fruit trees. Another golf cart was parked next to it.

"Hola Javier!" an older Hispanic man appeared in the doorway of the stable and approached us.

"Señor Tom! Buenas tardes. How are you?"

"Bien, y tu?"

Tom turned to me. "Maddie, this is Javier Martin del Pacifico. He's the caretaker for the horses and landscaper. Javier is a man of many talents and has become like part of your Aunt's family."

Tom handed me the envelope with Javier's name written on it.

"Maddie, you are supposed to present this to Javier."

I took the envelope and cautiously approached the man in the cowboy hat with the weathered face.

"This is for you."

Javier seemed nervous, he bowed slightly to me and carefully held it in his hands.

"I am Helen's grand niece." I looked back at Tom for assurance. He nodded to me.

"Don't be shy." I said , "You can open it."

He carefully tore the end off the envelope and pulled out a check. Tears welled in his eyes. He took his hat off and kissed my hand, "*Gracias*" he said over and over again

"So very nice to meet you. I miss your Tia Helen very much."

"Thank you Javier, it is also a pleasure to meet you."

Javier motioned us into the stable building.

"Señorita Maddie, I like you to meet Lucy and Ricky."

"Your aunt Helen was so proud of her horses." Tom added, "As you can figure out from their names, she was really into the *I Love Lucy* TV show, and those two older horses are Ethel and Fred." The two gray horses were in the back munching on hay, but Lucy stuck her head over the stall toward me while Ricky nuzzled Tom.

Javier smiled at me, "You ride Señorita?"

I nodded and stroked Lucy on the head.

Tom pulled his smartphone out and checked the time. "We're not going to be able to ride right now, but let's take a quick drive around the rest of the estate before I catch the boat back to the mainland."

As we made a big circle of the property I spotted a few sheep, and fruit trees covered with oranges, lemons, apples and avocados. He took me down near some cliffs that dropped off into the ocean. On the way back to the house we hit several big pot holes. Tom stopped and got out to see if the cart was damaged.

"Funny, I don't remember those holes when I was up here last month. Those are dangerous. Someone could get hurt"

Back at the house, he put his hand on my shoulder, "Again, my condolences for your Aunt Helen, my father worked with her before I came into the firm but I miss her very much." After a moment of silence he picked up his briefcase. "I'll be back next week with some tax paperwork."

I let out a big sigh that unfortunately he noticed.

"Sorry but it's necessary. We'll go for a horseback ride then."

An hour or so later the doorbell rang or at least I thought I heard it. Strange, I hadn't heard anyone drive up the road. Carefully, I opened the door. "Javier!"

He stepped into the foyer and slipped off his shoes. "Oh, you don't have to take off your shoes."

"I must, *Señorita*, they have much dirt."

"What can I do for you?"

"I did not know *Señora* Helen die until I see last week in newspaper. I am very sad." He pulled out the envelope I had given him from my Aunt and handed me the letter with the check stapled to it. "I don't understand so good. You read for me please?"

I read it aloud.

"From the law offices of... blah, blah blah, hmmmm. In the event of my death... blah, blah... as part of the disposition of my estate... Oh, here - This certified cashier's check in the amount of three hundred and fifty thousand dollars has been willed to my loyal employee and trusted friend Javier Martin del Pacifico for his many years of service, help and companionship. I am only sorry it could not be more, but I know of no price to put on friendship.

Note: Javier, Please take this money as a token of my thanks and go home to your family in Mexico where you are loved and surely missed. Signed, Your friend, Mrs. Helen Devine"

I folded the letter back up and placed it in his hands. Tears were rolling down his weathered cheeks and bouncing off the folds of his skin.

"So... Javier, Now you can go home a rich man."

"I no go home to Guadalajara."

"Why not? You can live very well on this for the rest of your life."

"No, I bring my wife and *niños* here to United States. Is better to be not so rich here than rich in Mexico."

He took my hand and kissed it. *"Muchisimas Gracias, Señorita."*

I escorted him to the front door. "Don't thank me. Thank *Señora* Helen in your prayers."

"Señora Helen, she is an angel, sí?"

Tears I'd been holding in leaked out all over my face. I didn't know coming to Catalina was going to make me feel so guilty for not knowing more about my aunt.

"Sí, Javier, an angel."

He stopped just outside he door, "Is okay if I still take care of *los caballos* - ah, horses? They are my other children."

"Whatever you like, Javier." I said, waving to him as he walked down the gravel drive.

As soon as he was gone, I went to Catalina Disposal. The gravel parking lot was empty, Luke was watching for me from the window. "Good you made it. You may want to go inside and put on these coveralls before you climb around in the trash."

I held the thing up - it was orange like the ones I see prisoners wearing on the TV news cleaning up the freeways.

"Hold out your arms." I did and he gave me a hard hat, hair net, disposable dust mask, and safety goggles." After I put them on I saw myself in the mirror on the back of the door.

"You have got to be kidding - this is a joke, right?"

"What's wrong? You don't want to get some nasty bug."

"Can I go look for the thing I lost now?"

"Not quite yet..." - he dropped a pair of knee high rubber boots on the floor in front of me and handed me a pair of huge yellow neoprene gloves that came to my elbows.

"Holy shit! Is this all really necessary?" I turned back around and saw a brilliant flash of light in my eyes. "Hey!? Did you just take my picture? I'll kill you Luke Garrett." Just then an older man with graying temples came out of a back office.

"What's all the noise Luke? I'm trying to make some phone calls and... What in God's name do we have here?" With a twinkle in his eye, he extended his hand, "Son, aren't you going to introduce us?"

"Oh sorry Dad, this is Maddie Van der Wald, Helen Devine's Grand Niece. She's living up at Dove Acres. Maddie, my father, Charles Garrett."

From inside my get up all he probably heard me say was, "plmmph mummph yu." I pulled my mask down, "A pleasure to meet you Mr. Garrett." I think that's what finally came out.

He chuckled, "I'm glad to meet some of Helen's family." and returned to his office shaking his head.

"Luke, I am never going to forgive you for this... ever!"

He walked me over to the dumpsters. "Just climb up that ladder on the end and hop in."

"Can't we open the big doors on the back instead of climbing in?"

"If I open up the back it will spill out and get mixed up with the others."

I pulled myself up the metal rungs on the side and peered down into the cavernous container when it dawned on me the only view Luke had was my butt.

"You could at least show me the best way to get in here... Luke!"

"Oh, okay. Hang on."

Once I got his attention away from my rear, he climbed up the other side and swung his legs around.

"Just swing your legs around and drop down onto a bag."

I did, landing on my back on top of a bunch of bags with pokey things in them. I was not happy. All the bags looked the same, so I tore one open. Papers, rags, old clothes dead flowers and old newspapers... no success. I tore open the next one, nothing.

"I could help you if I knew what you were looking for."

"All right. I'm looking for a silvery pin almost four inches across that looks like two overlapping leaves with...er...rhinestones or crystals all over it..."

Luke tore into one and found a shoebox full of a bunch of junky looking pins and other jewelry. He held up a big pin between this thumb and forefinger.

"Um...does this look like it?"

Quickly I grabbed it from his hand. With it tightly in my giant, yellow gloved hand I pulled my mask back down and planted a big kiss right on his lips.

"Well - um, thanks for your help."

"Okay," was all he said.

That's when I discovered there was no way to get out. I jumped up and down until Luke lifted me up high enough to grab the top edge. He put his palm squarely on my butt and pushed me to the top like he was making a basketball shot. I was so humiliated.

"May I please have that shoe box?"

He handed it up to me. With it tucked under my arm I climbed down the ladder and ran to my car, still wearing all that stuff, and got out of there as quickly as I could. But now I'll have to come back to return the dumb outfit. Maybe I'll just mail it.

Chapter Three

It was early and still dark when a noise woke me up. I tried to go back to sleep but there it was again. I pulled the blanket over my head. The house was old and I was sure it was just that. "Creak, rattle, Ohhhhhooo." Wait - even old houses don't go "Ooohhhoo!" It had to be ghost noises. I laid very still when I heard the doorknob jiggling. I wasn't going to lay here and be murdered like some bad slasher movie. I slipped quietly out of bed, grabbed my hairbrush and tiptoed to the door. If I was going to die - I was not going down without a fight. One deep breath and I jerked the door open. Jojo and I both screamed, and jumped back.

"Do you know what time it is?"

Jojo checked her indestructible, camp counselor watch, "Almost six-thirty a.m., and girl, you need to start locking things up around here. A city kid like you should know that."

I smacked her on the butt with my brush, "You scared the crap out of me!"

She held her hands up and said, "Whoooooo wants coffee?"

"Ha ha - real cute. Don't ever scare me like that again or, or.."

"Or what? You think you can kick my ass?"

I ignored her remark, threw on a pair of shorts and a t-shirt, and managed to follow her to her golf cart. Jojo was saying something, but my brain wasn't awake yet. We stopped in front of the Market in town to pick up a few things.

JoJo pushed me up to the counter. "Pinkie, this is Maddie Van der Wald. We're cleaning up her Aunt Helen's place."

The round, pink-faced lady's face lit up. She stopped, wiped her hands on a small white towel tucked in her apron and leaned against the register. "Well for goodness sake! You must be Madeline!" She looked me up and down while she tucked her silvery hair back into shape before coming around the counter to hug me. Who is Pinkie and how did she know my name? She must be an old friend of Aunt Helen.

"Uh, Pinkie..." I asked, looking at her name badge for reference, "Did you know my Great Aunt Helen?

"... Did I know your aunt? Hell, I'm Pinkie Wamsutta. You girls got a minute? - Raylene!" she shouted toward the back of the market. "I need you up front, pronto!"

The sound of cans tumbling to the floor and a distant "Just a second!" preceded Raylene as she bounced up the far left-hand aisle and appeared at Pinkie's side. She was a extremely hot blonde wearing sprayed-on red skinny jeans and a too-tight short-sleeved blue gingham blouse knotted under her perky but very grown-up boobs. She had to be younger than me, sixteen or a really good-looking eighteen. I couldn't help but glare at her and Jojo saw it. She let me know I was out of line by stepping on my foot. "Ow!"

"You okay Madeline?" Pinkie asked.

"Fine. I just bumped my knee on something."

Pinkie untied her apron, lifted it over her head and hung it on a wooden peg near the front door. Pointing her thumb toward the entrance, "Leave your stuff here" Raylene will watch it."

Miss perky boobs showed her dislike for babysitting our stuff by rolling her eyes and popping her gum.

"Follow me, CuppaJoe is just a short walk from here. It's new and the owner is a coffee wizard."

Pinkie took my arm, "It's just so good to finally meet you. Your Great Aunt Helen talked about you so much that I feel I already know you." I looked back and saw the blond watching us from the doorway with her hands on her hips.

"You know Helen came here as a young bride way before you were even born."

The Small tables at CuppaJoe lined the brick walls but they were taken.

Pinkie called back over her shoulder, "How about you girls? Would you like something?"

Jojo volunteered, "I'll have what you're having and a poppy seed lemon muffin, if they got any."

When the clerk pulled one out of the case Jojo practically drooled. "Maddie, you wanna split it?" Her eyes never left the muffin. I think she was feeling guilty.

"My treat," Pinkie insisted.

"Oh." Jojo replied, "Well then, what are you having Maddie?"

"Just herb tea and a biscotti, thanks."

We snagged a table by the window.

Pinkie took a sip of her drink, "As I was about to say, some of the old timers insisted your aunt and uncle weren't really Islanders let alone Californians, just because they inherited a bunch of land from your uncle's father on the backside of the island. Some people started rumors about buried treasure or that your uncle wanted to drill for oil. Somebody accused them of growing pot. The Sheriff even went up to check it out a couple of times, but it was all sour grapes, you know – jealousy."

Pinkie took a long sip on her straw and sighed,

"Your great uncle George bought a couple of saddle horses and some sheep. He thought the sheep could keep all the grass mowed, so he hired a young Mexican... Javier. Your aunt didn't like to drive that road from the house down to Avalon, so when George was out of town, Javier would drive her down to pick up the mail or go grocery shopping."

Pinkie sighed, stood up and looked out the door toward the market, "I better get back to the store pretty soon. Raylene's been acting very odd lately. I think she's got a boyfriend."

She sucked the rest of the coffee up through her straw, "So, if anyone gives you trouble, just let me know. Any of Helen's kin are my kin too, and be sure to take some empty cardboard boxes with you.

***

Back at Dove Acres, we were putting the boxes in the garage where Jojo saw something covered by an old throw rug. We pulled it off and found a wooden crate full old snorkeling stuff.

"Hey," Jojo said, "I got a couple free hours, let's go snorkeling." She picked up the crate and headed for her cart.

"Wait, Jojo I've never been snorkeling."

"Can you swim?"

"Yea, but..."

"If you swim you can snorkel. Period."

We drove down to the cliffs and walked down the narrow gravel path to the beach. At the bottom she sat down pulled two masks, swim flippers and snorkel tubes out of the crate that looked like no one had worn them for years. "Rubber's still good." JoJo declared.

"Shouldn't we disinfect them?"

"Where's your sense of adventure?" She pushed a mask and snorkel at me, "Put this one on." She pulled her shirt over her head and wriggled out of her shorts.

"What are you doing JoJo?" She took off her bra and slid her out of her underwear.

"I'm going snorkeling and I don't plan to get my clothes all wet. Besides, there's nobody around. Come on."

I looked all around for spectators before stripping down to my underwear.

"Come on!" Jojo yelled. "Don't be such a prude! Take it all off!"

"No way." I'm no prude! But I've never gone swimming in the ocean naked. I took one more look around before wedging my feet into the flippers and tripped along behind her into the crashing waves. She stuck the snorkel tube in her mouth and pulled the mask over her eyes. I figured if she can do it, so could I, and followed her lead.

Once I put my face underwater, I was seduced by the ocean. A whole new world appeared. The sun was warm and I forgot about the gross smell of old rubber and plastic. As I watched the kelp dance a waltz with the current. JoJo swam to me and pointed to a line of squarish boulders on the bottom. We followed them to the shore where JoJo pulled her mask up on her head and yelled over the crashing waves. "These aren't natural. Let's follow them and see where they go." The stones led us into a small cave. "The tide must be out," Jojo explained, "or this would all be under water."

I looked around the inside of the cave, "I'm sure lots of people have explored this place." The boulders stopped at a pile of small rocks at the back.

"Like I said," Jojo repeated, "this would all be under water if the tide was in."

A small wave washed over the small rocks making them clank and bang into each other.

"The tide probably piled those rocks on top of each other over the years." Wow, did I say that? I must've retained something from my earth science class in high school.

Jojo sprawled on the bed of smooth rocks. "This is the life, hiding in a cave and nobody can find us." I joined her and mentioned the book I was writing.

"Write? You never even liked to read."

"Ha ha – very funny. I'm writing a book, my great American novel. It takes place during the Revolutionary War. I can imagine my characters or even pirates hiding in a cave just like this."

"You never told me about any book, when did this start?"

"Well, I'm a quarter of the way done writing it. But I still have to do more research. Since I'll be stuck at Dove Acres for six months, I could finish my research online."

"Why the Revolutionary War? Why not Sci-Fi? You know, Martians or vampires and God knows anything you want?"

"After Mom and Dad died I was going through their stuff and learned Mom was a member of the Mayflower Society. I looked it up and found out she's related to a couple that came over on the Mayflower. I feel I need to honor her before I forget her."

Jojo was quiet.

"You want to help with the research? Jojo, she was your mother too you know."

"Not really..." I sensed she wanted to say more but something was stopping her. I stood up, "We should head back now."

"Let's stay longer," she protested, "it's too nice to leave," but she still followed me up the sandy trail to where we left the cart.

"Yoo-Hoo, Young ladies!" a voice called from somewhere in the distance. I searched for the source and spied a jet black bun of hair over the tall grass attached to a most unusual woman. She was waving her straw hat at us. Without any towels, Jojo's idea that we wouldn't get our clothes wet was a waste. We were soaked through and our hair was wet and matted.

"Hello there." The woman was dressed in a combination of gypsy fortuneteller, hippie and resort chic with giant hoop earrings dangling from her ears. As she walked her brightly colored necklace and bead bracelets clacked and rattled.

I must've looked like I'd just seen an alien as she got closer.

"Sorry if we're trespassing," Jojo said. "We were following a trail from the shore and ended up here."

"Never mind that." She squinted at my face. "I think I know you."

"I'm Madeline Van der Wald."

"For goodness sake! Maddie, you were just a little squirt the last time I saw you. And look how you've grown." She turned to Jojo and said, "and you must be Josephine. You've become quite a lovely young woman."

"Thanks, it's Jojo."

"For goodness sake, you probably don't even remember me. I'm Tanta Dimple. That's what you two used to call me. My real name is Dimple Outhouse, it's pronounced Aukhouse, but it's spelled like the privy." She brushed the dust and burrs off her skirt, "Your Aunt Helen talked about you all the time, and showed me every photo of you she received over the years. I feel as though I know you as well as my own daughter. Do you two have time to come up to the house for tea?"

I hesitated, feeling my wet pockets, "I'd rather go home and put on some dry clothes first."

"Well..." Dimple continued, "I'll just go start the water boiling. You change first if you want and come over, no need to knock and don't worry about your wet clothes, everything is wet around here anyway. See you in a jif." She scurried back up toward her house, black hair bun bouncing until she was out of sight.

Just then, I heard someone calling "Maddie! Maddie! I was worried for you!"

It was Javier.

"I think maybe you fall off a cliff or something. Where have you been?"

Jojo seemed relieved someone was concerned about us. "It's spooky up here isn't it Maddie? I mean you've got all these people popping up out of nowhere."

"*Señor* Tom call me on phone in the stable, he need to meet you tomorrow. It is okay *Señorita?*"

I nodded.

"Don't stay out too late, *Señorita*, it very dangerous here after dark."

In unison, "WHY?" we asked.

"You maybe fall from rocks and down on the waters. Be careful, okay? *Muy cuidado!*"

"Well what do you say Jojo? I have time for tea if it's okay with you."

"Sure, she sounds like a real kick!"

***

I threw our wet clothes in the dryer and gave Jojo some of my clothes to wear before we walked up the hill through the trees to the Outhouse mansion, a sprawling two-story structure with white wicker chairs on the broad porch.

"I never knew these places were up here!" JoJo admitted with amazement.

I called "Hellooo - it's us!"

"Make yourselves at home girls," Dimple chimed from somewhere upstairs, "I'll be right there."

She swept into the room carrying a steaming teapot in one hand, and in the other, a fancy silver tray. In one fluid motion she swooped toward the table depositing the teapot and the tray, which held three teacups, silver spoons, along with a plate of tea biscuits and little cucumber sandwiches.

"Tea and biscuits anyone?" Dimple poured hot tea into each cup, "Make sure you have some of the English tea biscuits." She handed me a linen napkin, a couple of the biscuits and a triangular cucumber sandwich with the crusts cut off.

"Enjoy, I'll just be a second." and disappeared through a doorway. She soon returned with an armload of photo albums.

"I've got to show you something..." Dimple rifled through the albums as if they were the telephone book, "It's in one of these." She stopped abruptly at one of the deckle edged, black and white photos held in place by tiny little black paper corner holders.

"Look." she sat back, and put her finger on the edge of the photo, as if she expected some sort of instant reaction from us.

I squinted at the image, "What am I looking at?"

JoJo gasped and covered her mouth as her eyes grew as big as saucers. "It's you Maddie! Look! It's you in that photograph!"

"Where?" I leaned in close. "I wasn't even born yet. How could I be in a picture that old!"

"That's the old S.S. Catalina, the great white steamer! Now look there in the front row." Dimple said. "It's your aunt Helen the day she arrived on Catalina Island. That's why I recognized you right off."

I didn't see the resemblance.

Dimple continued, "Honestly, at first I thought I saw a ghost. Your aunt was about twenty-three in this photo and you look just like her at that age." She showed us many more old photos of my aunt and her together.

"That is amazing! I appreciate that you shared all this with us, but we need to get back. Jojo is heading out to day camp tomorrow morning."

Dimple handed me an engraved calling card, "Here's my number, call me anytime and we'll get together for lunch or dinner sometime soon."

"Thanks Dimple." She gave us each a hug that reminded me of my mother. "I was afraid I'd be marooned alone out here!"

"Well Madeline, now we can be alone together."

Jojo and I walked back to the house. While we dodged more freshly dug holes on the way back home, she turned to me, "I was just wondering about this cousin who'd get this place if you didn't... Is he cute? Is he rich? or just dopey?"

"I don't know. Never met him. The lawyer said he lives in Missouri and I think he's several years older than me."

"Don't you think maybe inheriting all this instead of him is a blessing?"

I tried to hold back my emotions when she asked me that.

"A blessing? I don't know, I wish Mom and Dad were here to help me with all the business stuff."

"I'm sure they're proud of you for being brave and coming out here in the first place. You've stepped up and taken responsibility for yourself. That takes courage, girl."

"Thanks, but it just seems like everyone I care for has died – except you."

Chapter Four

Early the next morning I took a couple of the boxes Jojo labeled "photos" downstairs to the living room. I thought I could handle being here alone, but it's easy to get lonely.

In one of the boxes I found small photo albums and pictures of me as a child with people I didn't recognize. Beside each unknown face, I put a yellow sticky note. Maybe Pinkie or Dimple knows who they are.

There were a lot of faded black and white photos that must have been really old, like from the 1940s. Some vintage color photos from the 50s or 60s and a round plastic carousel of retro 1970's slides. Most were pictures of parties that were held right in this room. The fashions changed with each year. I looked up at the ten foot tall mirror with its gold borders that was in almost every shot. The newest photo had a little date stamp in the corner from last year and everyone was dressed in weird clothes. I didn't get it until I read the back, "New Years - Come as you were party." I put the box on the table and took some more old clothes and stuff to the garage. After a while the trash bags and boxes began to pile up. Once again I felt the familiar ground shaking rumble of Luke's dumpster truck.

"I'm going to have to get a gate with an intercom or something," I mumbled to the door before I opened it. "People just show up without warning."

Luke was standing on the front step, all washed up clean, looking at the garden with his Giants cap in his hand.

"What are you doing here?" I asked. "Did I forget to sign my check?"

"No, I had to do something and I was in the area." He produced a bouquet of wildflowers from behind his back. He must have picked them along the road on the way here.

"I'd like to start over since our first meeting wasn't exactly friendly."

"...or our second for that matter." I reminded him.

He smiled and put out his hand. "Hello, I'm Luke Garrett."

"I'm pleased to meet you Mr. Garrett. His hands were rough and callused. "Thanks for the flowers, they're pretty."

"How'd you like to have lunch today?"

"What? You mean like a date? This is kind of soon - I mean we just met a minute ago."

"It's not a date. I'm just trying to be neighborly and welcome you to the island."

"Whatever... I can't today, I have a meeting with my aunt's lawyer."

"Well what about tomorrow?"

"I don't know yet. I'll check my calendar and call you." That was a lie, but I didn't want to seem needy.

"Fine." He opened the door of his truck, "So, what are you gonna do out here all by yourself?"

"I'm writing a novel, and without a lot of distractions, I might get it finished."

"I've never met an author before, I'm impressed."

"Well don't be, I'm not an author yet and I have lots of research to do."

"So lunch tomorrow?"

I shrugged and nodded. "I'll think about it."

"I'll call tomorrow." He started his truck and rumbled down the road.

Since I've told practically everyone that I was working on my novel, I better set up my laptop in the kitchen and unpack my notes. I've been here less than a week but it feels like a year.

When I opened my binder a note fell out: "Did Americans have chocolate in the eighteenth century?" I did an online search and found links about the history of cocoa. I read the ones that looked interesting... until I heard a car.

"Tom!" I almost forgot he was coming. I looked at myself in the mirror as I headed for the door. Well, shorts and t-shirt better be okay. Through the window I saw him getting out of a jeep, so unlike the first time he came here. No suit. Instead he had on khaki cargo shorts and a long sleeved tee.

"Hey," he said as he walked right to the kitchen and peeked at my laptop screen open on the counter.

"I was researching chocolate in the colonies during the eighteenth century. Any idea if it was around?"

He shrugged, "Why is that important?"

"Research for my novel." I politely closed the lid of my laptop before he read too much.

"Are you ready to go for that ride?"

"Now?" I glanced back at my computer, "Sure, I guess."

We hopped into the jeep and drove to the stables where Javier had Lucy and Ricky already saddled.

Tom pulled a couple of carrots out of his pocket for the horses, handed one to me for Lucy while he offered the other one to Ricky. The horses munched down the carrots and nudged us for more, "Sorry, Lucy," I stroked her head, "That's all I have." She jerked her head up and turned to get a drink from the big watering trough.

After trotting around the stable area we headed to the cliffs, Tom pointed down at the water's edge, "At one time that beach belonged to your family but it's public now. The property line is at the high tide mark."

We watched the ocean crash along the shore below as a breeze came up blowing my hair.

Tom pointed off in the distance, "Your aunt was considering putting a cell phone repeater tower up right by the stable. She could have made a steady two or three grand a month. But then she passed." He paused. "I liked your aunt very much. She was a family friend for decades. My father was their lawyer, now I am. Unfortunately, times change and so do circumstances.

We rode off to the east through the flat land and over a small knoll. With clear blue skies and a warm breeze from the south, it couldn't have been a nicer afternoon. We crested the hill where I spotted a small gazebo under a tree. Tom rode ahead of me. A folding table was set up along with a cooler chest.

I reined Lucy back, "Luncheon is served." Tom reached up to help me dismount and had me sit where I could see the ocean while he brought out sandwiches, fruit and juice from the cooler.

"Wow. This is a surprise."

"I wanted to welcome you to Dove Acres..." He placed two glasses on the table and filled each one with apple cider, "in the proper Helen DeVine style."

We toasted.

"Your uncle was crazy about Helen his whole life. My father told me George hated to travel alone and fretted about Helen until he got home again."

I could imagine my aunt and uncle sitting here enjoying the life they'd made together.

"While you've been up here, have you thought about income for yourself?"

"I came here to write my book in peace but in the short time I've been here, I haven't had much chance. I was thinking about the possibility of converting this place to a Bed and Breakfast Inn and maybe offer horseback riding and at the bottom of the cliffs... I could rent boats. It seems a shame no one knows about this place. It's just beautiful."

"It is lovely." Tom responded. "There's nothing between here and Hawaii. Maddie those ideas of yours will take capital you don't have yet. The cell tower I mentioned is a short term solution that will start making money for you within a few months. The Bed and Breakfast idea, while a great use of the land will take years to prepare. As things are now, I can't see how you will last more than a month or so before the wolves will be hounding you for back taxes, property tax and the like."

He made sense about the tower and maybe it will be a good idea to get money rolling in while I finish my book.

"I typed up a list of companies for your aunt that you should consider. It's in the car. I'll leave it for you before I go."

Dealing with a bunch of boring business stuff was not my idea of a way to spend my summer. I just wanted to have a chance to write.

"I still have my parent's life insurance. Maybe I can use that, finish my novel and keep Dove Acres going until then, maybe sell the property. Then I can get back to my life on the mainland."

"You really don't want to use all that insurance and inheritance money at this stage of... you're not even twenty one yet. You have college and your whole life ahead of you."

"You sound just like my father, 'Maddie, you have to go to college.' But where better to be inspired than here at Dove Acres?"

Tom didn't bring up any business for the rest of lunch, but he left me the list of companies and some tax forms to read and sign. I wasn't thrilled about reading any of it and stuffed them in my purse.

As he got back into the Jeep he reminded me, "I'd like you to think about the cell tower. You're going to need a reliable source of income to keep this place afloat." He pointed a finger, "Think hard about it."

I should have thanked him for all of his attention and I could have used a fatherly hug right then, but I restrained myself. Sometimes it seems like Tom wants to take care of me and other times it feels kind of creepy. Maybe it's because he's a lot older than me. I glanced at the list of companies he said would be interested in putting up the tower, but I really didn't want to think about it yet, so I went back to my online chocolate research when I heard a faint knocking from downstairs. Maybe living in this big empty house is getting to me. There it was again. I definitely heard knocking. For being stuck out here away from Avalon there are sure a lot of people around. "I gotta get a gate and that security system put in." I said out loud. All the weird noises around here were getting on my nerves and I'm talking to myself. There it was again. I looked out the window but didn't see anyone at the front door, so I trotted down the stairs to see who knocked. I'd be pissed if it was like, some religious missionaries or something. When I pulled open the big front door. Nobody was there. "Hello?" I called... nothing. A knocking came from the kitchen door. I locked the front door and went to the back. Through the window on the door, I saw that nobody was there. Just to be sure, I opened the kitchen door and looked both ways - no one. I threw my hands up and started for the stairs. If Jojo is pulling another ghost prank on me, she is gonna pay for it. The doorbell rang. I flung the door open, ready to grab her but standing on my front step was a small boy and an even smaller girl with dimpled faces and wide-eyes. He winced when I jumped into the doorway and she started to cry. "Oh – I'm sorry. I didn't mean to scare you guys."

The boy answered, "I wathn't theared." He put his arm around the little girl. He couldn't have been more than five or six years old and she looked about three or four. The boy had a long handled butterfly net that reached a foot above his head, while the little curly haired girl sniffled and held out a coffee can with holes punched in the plastic lid. On a paper label taped to the front of the can, written in bright green letters was one word - "BUGS." They both smiled up at me. I squatted down to their level, "Why hello there. What can I do for you?" I glanced up to look behind them for an adult or older kid. As far as I could tell there was no one else.

The boy raised up his net and asked, "Do you need any bugth catched?" the little girl nodded vigorously in agreement and held up the can so I could see the label.

"Well, how much is this going to cost me?"

The boy held up two fingers, "Only two dollarth."

"That's very reasonable. Do you live around here?"

Simultaneously they pointed behind them toward the road. "Ober dare." the little girl replied.

"Does you mommy know where you are?"

"She inna car waitin' for uth by doze twees."

"My, that's far away. You can look for bugs here by my flower garden and I'll go talk to your mommy, okay?" They nodded and ran around the house with their net and can. As they did, I could hear the little girl pleading with the boy, "Can I get thum too? Can I?"

I smiled and walked down the road. It warmed my heart to imagine what Dove Acres would be like with the sound of little children running around the house.

Just as they said, I found their mommy sitting in an old, dented Jeep Wagoneer with all the windows open parked under a tree.

"Hello?" I called.

She stepped out of the Wagoneer with a baby blanket covering her shoulder.

"Hi, I'm Maddie Van der Wald, are you the little bug catchers' mommy?"

"I hope they aren't bothering you. Mrs. Devine let them come up here last fall to catch bugs and go swimming in her pool. She's such a sweet lady... always gives them a little something for catching the bugs. Makes them feel proud and useful."

My chest felt heavy as I found myself forced to say, "You didn't know? Mrs. DeVine, passed away almost four months ago."

She flipped back the blanket, revealing a sleeping baby.

"Oh Lord, No I didn't. Four months ago? That was just before little April here was born. That's so awful... I'm very sorry, we didn't mean to impose on you... I'll go get Nicholas and Sarah." She walked past me and started toward the house with the baby over her shoulder.

"It's okay, I'm her niece."

She stopped.

"C'mon," I urged, "let's go see how those two are doing and have some tea. We can keep an eye on them from the dining room."

"That would be very nice. I hope we're not imposing."

"It's totally fine, by the way, what's your name?"

"I'm sorry. How rude of me." She stuck a hand out from under the blanket, "Veronica Christensen."

I unlatched the French doors in the dining room and let them swing wide with the ocean breeze.

"Nicholas...Sarah," she called, "I'm in here."

"Hi mommy," they waved to her.

"You have such cute children. How long have you lived on the Island?"

"Not quite a year. Since I was about four months pregnant with April."

Her baby began to fuss. "I'm going to have to feed her. I hope you don't mind if I nurse her."

I shook my head, "I hope this isn't too personal, but what brought you here?"

"It's okay. I brought my two kids here to get away from my nutjob second husband, I should say soon-to-be ex-husband, after my first husband, Jared passed away."

She looked awfully young to be a widow. "What happened?"

"Jared was diagnosed with an aggressive cancer. We struggled with his disease for several months which used up our medical insurance benefits and all our savings. We had to sell our beautiful home in Newport Beach, both our cars, and even exhausted the children's college funds on medical bills, surgeries and trips to specialists. But God let him die anyway, leaving me with those two little angels."

"I'm so sorry. You had to be very strong and brave to get through that."

"Thanks. What else could I do? I mourned for a while, but you know, Jared and I had five great years together, so when we knew he was going to die, we had no regrets. We had our chance to say goodbye. He even videotaped a message for each of the children while he still looked good. I'll play it for them someday when they are old enough to understand."

"You said he was your first husband?"

She nodded and took another look outside for her kids while she wiped a stray tear from her cheek.

"I got involved with a few cancer support groups on the internet while he was sick and kept up the online friendships I made after his death. A woman in one of the chat rooms for families of cancer victims told me about Internet dating, so I tried it a few months. I didn't know there were so many pathetic losers in the world... well, I should talk. I mean, look at me and my children, we're living in that junker of a car, for goodness sake. Anyway, I met this guy online. He said was a Christian and already had three kids of his own, and said he'd lost his spouse like me. After writing back and forth for a while, we got together and dated a few times, then we got married."

I was amazed by her story and by the way she could talk for minutes on end, apparently, without breathing. I guess she just needed to talk. I could identify with her after being up here alone, even for a short time.

"This guy talked a really good story, and treated me pretty well while we dated, but as soon as the ring was on my finger, he changed. I'm talking, as soon as that thing slipped over my knuckle - at the reception, he got drunk, and bossy, he pulled out a cigar to celebrate - I didn't even know he smoked. Then a couple weeks after the honeymoon, he wanted me to do all sorts of weird things like illegal drugs and sex with other women. I refused. He turned into a regular freakazoid. Even if I was open to kinky things like that, there were five kids in the house. He kept telling me he was coming into a lot of money, real soon. But I couldn't handle it. He didn't treat my kids as well as his. He was always drunk, and abusive. He was a mean drunk, he'd yell at Nicholas and hit him. He'd stay out every night and sometimes he didn't come home at all, probably chasing other women. Except for our wedding day, he never went to church with me or the kids. A Christian - Hah. The big fat liar. I just couldn't take it anymore, so one night four months later, while he was out drinking, I took my two babies and went to a safe house for abused women and their children. I didn't even know I was pregnant with April until a couple months after I got away. We've been running ever since. I filed for divorce, but the attorney said he wouldn't sign the papers. So, until he signs – I'm still legally stuck with the jerk. I should've known better than to trust someone on the Internet.

She took a sip of her tea, "It was all a big mistake I'd like to forget, so I went back to my first husband's name - Christensen. I figured Catalina Island would be the last place the other guy would ever look for us. I got a room at the Atwater Hotel and a job at the video arcade, but it closed and they made an Italian restaurant out of it. Like there aren't enough Italian restaurants in this world. I applied for a job with the new owners but they didn't hire me. They said I didn't have the look they wanted. I think it's because they didn't want a pregnant waitress, so I got unemployment for a while, then April was born."

"You had your baby alone?"

She nodded. "But when I got to the medical clinic, everyone was very supportive."

I can't imagine doing something like that and wondered what I would do.

"Where do you and your children stay?"

She hugged her nursing baby, "We just cuddle up together in the Wagoneer during the mild season. The people here have been really good to us. Mr. Garrett Sr. at the recycling place is pretty generous and sometimes gives me little extra when I bring in recyclable stuff so we can get a room when it gets cold. Pinkie Wamsutta lets us park in back of the market - out of the wind and she gives us day old bread to go with our peanut butter and jelly. And you know, the churches here help us out a lot too. We'll get through this."

I was feeling very guilty after hearing her story, and all this time I've been whining about how tough my life is.

"You know, Veronica, I have this big house and a couple spare rooms. I've been busy doing an inventory of my aunt's things, organizing her affairs, and working on my book. If you could help me with work around the place, you and the kids can stay here until we can find a job for you and get you back on your feet."

I could see she'd had a hard life. There was beauty under the dirt. "Well? How do you feel about that?"

I think she was feeling ashamed to say yes, but what other choice did she have? She used to be a Newport Beach wife after all and still had a bit of pride.

She shook her head, "I really appreciate your offer, but you don't even know me and I don't want to impose."

I looked at her in disbelief. Was she turning me down?

"Are you sure?" I asked.

She looked away, nodded and called to her kids. "Nicholas, Sarah, come on in!" They came running to the house with their can of bugs.

"I'd like you to think about it Veronica and let me know. I've got plenty of room."

She stood, "Thanks for the tea and letting my children play but we have to go."

The little ones waved as she herded her little ones to the front door.

When did I get to be such a softy? What was I thinking - offering to take in a strange, homeless woman and three little kids? I gave them two dollars and seventy five cents each for catching bugs and watched them walk back to their car. My life was never, ever that bad, but if I don't do something about getting money coming in, it could be.

While I picked up the tea dishes and brought them to the kitchen, I imagined Veronica with her three little kids, sleeping in that old junker. She'll probably park under a tree someplace, or behind Pinkie's Market. I could just see Nicholas and Sarah curled up next to her and April in her arms.

After putting the cups and saucers in the dishwasher, I heard the doorbell again. "Here we go again." I mumbled, "Where are all these people coming from?" I dried my hands and answered the door.

Standing on my front step in tears was Veronica with her children.

"Only for a couple of weeks..." She insisted, "Okay? I'm only doing it for my children. If it was just me, I would've still said no. But I have a baby and my little ones to think of."

"It's a deal. May I hold April?"

She handed me her little daughter.

"Bring your things in and let's get a couple of rooms fixed up, then we can have dinner about - what? six-thirty? Is that okay?"

Veronica nodded and sobbed, "My children and I thank you for this."

"By the way," I asked, "All I have is some microwave diet dinners in the freezer, unless you know how to cook."

"Well, yes. I took a few classes at the Culinary Institute of America before I got pregnant with Nicholas. Once I had dreams of being a gourmet chef and having a little bistro on Balboa Island, but..." She shrugged, "When Jared died, so did my dreams."

"You're a chef? You really can cook? God bless you."

In my head, all I could think about was... she cooks, she cooks, she cooks.

As she scooped her other two children up in her arms and hugged them tight, I thought, "I know I'm doing the right thing and I'm glad someone's here to share the nights in this big house."

***

The next day Luke arrived for lunch a little early with his usual big smile. "It's been a while since I've been in the mansion." He remarked, "I gotta tell you, Helen's holiday party last year was a real kick." He peeked in the living room and perused the large mirror on the wall. "It's just as impressive as the last time I was here."

On the way to town, Luke gave me a quick tourist speech on island history. "Buffalos roamed the island for a while when movies were made here in the 1930's. The movie company had them shipped over for the Native American scenes to make them more authentic. Now there's only a few left."

"Native Americans - here?"

"I learned from the staff at the Catalina Museum figured a branch of the Tongva tribe lived here and traded with tribes on the mainland. That must've been a rough canoe ride."

We stopped by Antonio's, a nice seafood restaurant on the waterfront between the pier and the Tuna Club. Our table was under an awning facing the harbor. I'd eaten dinner there, but it looked completely different in the daylight.

"Have you decided what you want to do with all that land?" Luke asked as we scanned the menu.

I looked out at the horizon, "Well, I don't know, maybe a B&B or a resort. It already has a tennis court and an empty swimming pool. The stable has four horses I could include horseback riding, and maybe even hang gliding off the cliffs for the guests. ...Or maybe a spa, or even a golf course... I'd have to do some rearranging of the land for something like that, but it's going to take money. My lawyer suggested renting out part of the land and putting up a cell phone tower so I can get some money coming in.

"What? Maddie you can't go tearing up this island for commercial development and for all things a cell phone tower. The ecosystem would be destroyed! Don't you see the trouble already caused by all the development on the island..." He stopped and took a deep breath.

What was that all about? He didn't have to go off on me. If he didn't want to know my opinion, he shouldn't have asked. Anyway who did he think he was, trying to tell me what to do with my property. I sat silently and stared at my plate for the rest of lunch.

"I'm sorry Maddie, I was out of line. You're new to the island and you have a right to do what you want with your property."

I looked up, "I'm glad you changed your mind."

"I wouldn't put it that way but I need to be less...well less nosy." He quickly changed the subject, "So have you been on the water yet?

"I've been to the cliffs and shore on the north side."

"That's a popular spot for surfers, the die-hard ones anyway. Listen, I live on a boat. How'd you like to go for a sail sometime? The sunsets out here are really pretty and when it gets dark, we can watch the flying fish."

"Why do you live on a boat? Don't you live with your father?"

"It works out better this way. We don't always see eye-to-eye on a lot of things like the environment and global warming, so I live on the family's boat."

"Wait just a minute..." I must have looked like he tried to tell me the Easter Bunny was real. "... did you say FLYING fish?"

"What do you say? Would you like to go sailing sometime?"

"I don't know.... telling me there are flying fish out here sounds totally desperate."

He put his fork down. "You were born in Southern California and you've never heard of flying fish?"

I held my napkin to my mouth and shook my head, trying to keep from laughing.

"Nice try Mister Garrett. I'll have to give you extra points for originality."

He stared at me in disbelief.

"Do you think I'm trying to...? You think I'm lying!"

Looking around he spotted the server and called her over.

"You aren't going to give up are you? How dumb do you think I am anyway?"

Luke read the server's name tag, cleared his throat and said calmly, "Crystal, could you help me?"

"My name's not Crystal."

"That's what it says on your tag."

"Crystal took off with the soft drink delivery guy. They gave me her name tag until mine comes in. My name's Ashley."

"Well Ashley." Luke patiently said, "My friend here doesn't believe there are flying fish right out there - - Go ahead, tell her."

Luke waited for a response while I continued to hold my laughter in my napkin.

"Well Ashley? Go on, tell her."

She gave Luke a deer-in-the-headlights look, "Flying fish? There are fish that fly out here? That's really weird, I've never heard of flying fish. Are you jerking my chain?"

"How long have you lived in Avalon?" he asked impatiently.

Ashley glanced at me laughing in my napkin and turned back to Luke.

"Me? I'm from Bakersfield. I moved here two days ago. Yesterday was my first day on the job."

"Thanks Crystal, I mean Ashley, you been a BIG help." Frustrated, he rolled his eyes and turned back to me, "Take a flying fish cruise from the pier if you don't believe me.... wait. Here's an idea, go to the museum at the Casino. There's a whole display about flying fish, or ask anyone in town, Pinkie, Dimple... or call JoJo."

I dabbed the tears from my eyes in an attempt to appear serious. "It's not that I don't trust you, Luke, but I think I'll take a rain check on your offer and visit the museum first."

Luke twirled a bit of pasta on his fork and looked up at me in frustration, "Whatever."

"What are you smiling about?"

"I'm just imagining your face when you find out just how silly you've been. In fact, I have a proposition for you..."

This didn't sound very good.

"And what might that be?"

"What do you say to this? If you prove me wrong about the flying fish, and it turns out I'm just making fun of a tourist from the mainland, namely you... I'll come to your place and wash all the windows at your house - inside and out."

"All the windows?..." That old saying about offers that are too good to be true was ricocheting around in my head.

"...And if *I'm* wrong?"

"Then you'll have to spend a weekend with me on my boat watching the flying fish."

I set my glass down on the table and sat straight up. I don't think I'm wrong about this. Flying fish *indeed*, how naive does he think I am? Or did I miss something in biology class? I couldn't let him know I doubted myself. Could there be such a thing as flying fish? or was this whole thing an island conspiracy to make the city girl look foolish? In my most business-like tone, I said, "I'll take your deal," and extended my hand. He laughed, shook my hand, "Okay, but only because you insisted."

After dessert he suggested a walk along the water. I had a feeling he was up to something so I declined.

"Have you had a chance to enjoy your private cove?"

I told him about my lunch with Tom the day before and the cave Jojo and I found.

"A cave? Hah. What do you say we take a closer look at your cave?"

I looked back at the harbor, "Damn!"

"What?" Luke turned to me, "Did I say or do something? Have I got lipstick on me again?" joking.

"No... I think - I just saw something out there."

"Maybe," he smirked, "it was a flying fish."

"Very funny." I looked at Luke, "Let me ask you a question, you live aboard a sailboat in the harbor - right? Is that going to be a permanent thing? You plan to stay on the island the rest of your life? I mean, living on a boat seems temporary."

I hoped he hadn't seen this for what it was, an attempt to see if he was going to be around a while. After all, I could get emotionally or even physically involved and wake up one morning to find his boat and him gone - Poof.

"Well," he replied. "I used to think it was temporary up until about a day ago."

"What life changing event happened a day ago?"

"I met you." His eyes locked onto mine. Was that some kind of a lame pickup line? I tried to lighten the mood a bit, "I'm sure that I'm not the only reason you would want to stay here. Catalina is charming, historic, and you have a practically endless supply of trash from all the visitors."

Luke swallowed again, "Actually, your arrival on Catalina inspired my decision to stay."

"Is that so?" I had to change the subject, "So you think a B&B is a good idea?"

"The B&B could be a great thing, but the cell tower... I don't think is such a good idea."

"Look, I need something to keep Dove Acres from bankruptcy, and I can't throw my entire inheritance into it. I think it's a good beginning. Besides I didn't ask you for your opinion about the tower, I asked about the B&B."

"Maddie, you just can't build something like that here! This place needs to be left as is, maybe as a wildlife refuge or a reserve. For God's sake, those are the ONLY acceptable solutions in my opinion!" He calmed down and took another deep breath. "The B&B could be a wise choice as long as you don't build up the property too much. Just refurbish that fantastic house and move forward."

"Hey! Now wait a minute - all I did was ask a simple question. I haven't made a decision yet. Besides, it *is* my property and I can do what ever I want with it."

"People like you don't understand, there isn't enough water and every bit of trash has to be recycled because there aren't any viable landfills."

"Wait a minute. What do you mean by people like me?"

"I'm just saying that the good people of the island wanted me to replace the old incinerator with a new one, but I wouldn't. Burning pollutes the air, even the newest cleanest ones produce greenhouse gasses. I told them there are alternatives to incinerators. They should get down on their knees and thank God that my father and I came to this rock or they'd all be swimming around in their own filth!"

"I need to go home." I walked toward Pinkie's.

Luke followed me, but stopped in front of a shop window and stared, probably to admire himself. "Enjoying the view?"

He whipped his head around, stared at me and bolted around the corner. I sat on the bench in front of Pinkie's Market and looked out at the harbor. My Aunt and Uncle had each other and didn't have to make these kinds of decisions alone.

After a few minutes I was getting a little chilly when the breeze picked up. Luke came up behind me. "I want to apologize for ruining a wonderful afternoon."

Luke sat down beside me. "Please let me take you home. I shouldn't have gotten on my soapbox. It's a personality flaw I'm working on."

I took his hand. "At least you're passionate about something besides money."

"Maybe we can try lunch again tomorrow - my treat."

After Luke dropped me off I wandered into the kitchen and found a note taped on the fridge, "Maddie - I took the kids with me to Avalon for some groceries - be back soon. Veronica." So, I pulled a quart of Death by Chocolate out of the freezer and grabbed a tablespoon all the while wondering how I could have been so stupid and naïve. Luke is all about his precious island and furry things that live in holes. I stuck the spoon into the container and was about to call Dimple to arrange a picnic lunch for the next afternoon, when a noise came from outside. "Veronica? Is that you?" I shouted. Silence. "Is somebody there?" Immediately, I ran around the house double-checking the locks on all the doors and windows. That reminds me, I should ask Javier about those holes. After I was securely locked in, I went into the library and the scanned the floor-to-ceiling bookshelves, finally I plopped down in a big cozy leather armchair with one of my guilty pleasures, a Jill Landis romance novel, wrapped an afghan around me and switched on the bronze based Tiffany lamp. But instead of opening the book, I took out my cell phone to call Jojo. Just as I was punching in the number, I remembered my cell service didn't cover that side of the island.

"Shit."

I squirmed around until I found a comfortable position and opened the novel. I don't remember getting sleepy but I closed my eyes, just to rest them for a moment...

"Maddie. Maddie wake up."

The sound of two little voices woke me. I got one eye open but little fingers pushed the other one open. Nicholas and Sarah ran to the kitchen, "Mommy, Mommy, aunt Maddie is awake now." She carried April with her to where I was sprawled in the chair. My ice cream was now room temperature chocolate yuck.

Chapter Five

The sky was dark, no view of the ocean, no stars to wish by, just gray fog so thick the windows looked liked they were painted on the other side with gray paint. I poked my head out the front door to check the porch light. Then I heard it. A scraping, digging sound. If I called out, my voice would surely wake the children. There it was again. I grabbed my flashlight and pointed it in the direction of the sound but the fog swallowed up the beam of light. Quickly I locked the door and made another round of checking all the windows and doors before I went up to my room. This house was beginning to creep me out.

All night I tossed and turned with thoughts of strange noises. Luke, the legal stuff with Tom, and flying fish just added to the things that kept me up. I finally drifted off and when I woke up it was dawn. I'd hardly slept. Cereal and milk, my comfort food would make me feel better. With bowl in hand, I plodded back upstairs while shoveling crunchy spoonfuls into my mouth only to be surprised at the top of the steps by the smiling faces of Nicholas and Sarah. Veronica came out of her room toweling off her hair.

"Veronica." I must've really been groggy because I'd forgotten they were here.

"Did you hear the doorbell or was that my alarm clock? I thought I turned it off before it could buzz."

"I heard it too." She replied, "Who was it?"

I shrugged and shoved another spoonful of cereal into my mouth. Veronica shook her hair loose and said, "I was going to make breakfast for all of us, but I see you already started."

I held the bowl high turning around while the two little ones circled my legs and rushed past me down the stairs.

"Hey you two - Slow down." Veronica scolded.

I followed her down to the kitchen. At once she had coffee brewing, bacon cooking and bread in the toaster, all while she whipped up eggs for an omelet. Even though I wasn't hungry, I just had to have some.

It was so nice to have people, big and little to share my morning.

She stocked the freezer with meals she cooked ahead and kept me company until Luke showed up for our afternoon outing to the mysterious cave.

I was grateful the sun finally came out as I followed him down the dusty road past the stable with a picnic lunch made by Veronica. From there we hiked down the winding path to the beach. Luckily the tide was out. I took off my shoes to let the cool sand squish between my toes. Inside the cave we found the bed of small smooth rocks Jojo and I discovered earlier. The midday sun reflected off the water into the cave, lighting up the ceiling and walls. Luke made a place for the two of us to sit. The rocks felt cool and damp on my rump, and actually quite comfortable. I looked in the basket Veronica gave us and found some little smoked salmon sandwiches, cheese and two small bottles of sparkling mineral water. While we snacked Luke fidgeted around and finally pulled something from under the rocks, "Hmmm., look at this. It looks like a carved shell, maybe an arrowhead or spear tip for fishing." He found several others the same shape and size and held them up to the light.

Soon the fog rolled back in and the cave quickly got very dark. We barely made it to the top of the cliff before it was too foggy to see. I have to admit it was scary.

As we got closer to the house we both smelled the wonderful aroma of something baking.

Luke sniffed the damp air. "What smells so good? Do you have something cooking?"

"I met a really nice lady and decided to let her and her little family stay with me for a while."

"You're all alone here. Do you think it was smart to let strangers stay in your house?"

"Why not? She seems perfectly nice and her little kids are so cute." I pushed the front door open we were met by Veronica wearing an apron and oven mitts, "Hey Luke."

He looked at me and whispered, "This is really nice of you Maddie."

"Come into the kitchen." She wiped her hands on her apron, "I want you to taste something."

My mouth was already watering. On the kitchen island, a large baking sheet filled with pastry was cooling.

"I just made some cinnamon pecan rolls."

She sent Luke and me into the library and brought us a plate piled high with piping hot rolls drizzled with icing. "Here's some tea for you two. Enjoy, I've got little ones to look after."

A few minutes later Veronica stepped into the room and flopped into a big chair next to us. "Whew. The kids are finally all down for their naps." She leaned back and closed her eyes. Luke and I thought she was going to drift off to sleep when she sat bolt upright.

"It's been a long time since I've felt as welcome and secure as I do. I mean, my kids have warm soft beds to sleep in and Maddie, you've been so generous opening your home to us."

Luke seemed uncomfortable with all this female bonding, stood.

"Uh - I better get back to work. It's getting, uh... I better get back."

He gave Veronica a pat on the shoulder, "Glad to see you and your kids are okay. I've got some clothes that I picked up at the Thrift store for the baby. I'll drop them by tomorrow."

"No need for you to bring them up here," I said as we walked to the door, "I'll stop by your office and pick them up."

After a good night's sleep, I drove to the post office, picked up my mail then walked over to buy a few things at the market.

When I got back to my car I found my left front tire flat. That was very weird because I just checked them. I walked the couple blocks back from the water to the local garage. The mechanic came out to greet me, "So, what can I do for you?"

"I've got a flat tire. My car's only a couple blocks away. I'll show you."

He wiped his hands and followed me. "What kinda cart is it?"

"It's not a cart, it's a regular car – a 1965 Mustang."

"Oh, you must be Helen's niece."

I'd gotten used to the local fame, but I still wondered, "How'd you know? Did someone pin a sign on my back?"

He pointed at the name on his shirt, "I'm Al - Alfred and that's the only '65 Mustang on the island. I serviced it since I was old enough to work."

He squatted down and ran his hands around the tires, "Looks like someone punched a hole in the sidewall. We'll have to replace it. Do you have a spare?"

I popped the trunk and found a very old, very flat spare tire.

"Hmm, I guess you don't." he peered over my shoulder into the trunk. "I'll have to order two new tires from the mainland. They can be here tomorrow on the first boat."

"Two?"

"Yup... two. One for the flat on the car and one for the flat in the trunk."

"Shit, I mean excuse me but this is not turning out to be a very good day." I left my keys with Al and stopped for a chocolate ice cream cone by the waterfront where I plopped down on a bench feeling sorry for myself. All the tourists seemed happy, walking hand in hand with someone they cared for, and here I sat with a flat tire and no way to get back home except walk. I didn't want to call Veronica. She'd have to dress the kids, pack them up and haul them down here.

"Isn't that the best ice cream ever?" A stereo greeting perked up my ears.

I looked up and saw a double image of a beautiful, red haired woman with perfect hair and makeup standing in front of me. I put my head back and rubbed my eyes. "Jeez," I said. "Must be too much sun or I'm having a stroke."

"Don't worry, you're fine... we're twins." one said. "Identical twins," added the other.

I slowly opened one eye and looked at the trees, then straightened up and made eye contact with the voice.

One woman chirped, "My name's Jimmi Outhouse," followed by the other, "I'm Jonnie. Are you visiting for the day?"

I extended my hand and replied, "No. I'm Maddie Van der Wald and you two *must be* related to Dimple Outhouse."

The twins swiveled their heads to face each other, and back at me. "She's our aunt." They replied in unison with a smile. "You know her?"

"We met a couple of days ago. I'm your aunt Dimple's new neighbor...." the puzzled look stayed on their faces. "My late aunt was Helen Devine..."

"Oh!" They jumped up and squealed, "That is so cool." Jimmi was quivering with excitement. "We must have lunch." Jonnie leaned over and whispered something in her sister's ear. "Sorry for being so insensitive. Please accept our condolences for your loss. We knew Mrs. Devine quite well."

"Thanks, you're very nice. Are you on your way to visit your Aunt Dimple?"

"Yes, we just got off the boat, but it's a surprise." Jonnie whispered to me. "She hasn't seen us in more than a year."

"We've been traveling since graduation." Jimmi added. Jonnie followed with, "I was on a Mediterranean cruise with my boyfriend. I even brought her a little gift." She pointed to a large oddly shaped item, wrapped in newspaper sitting on the sidewalk.

Jimmi chimed in, "I was with my boyfriend and his family in Australia. Luckily we had time for a side trip to Fiji. He travels a lot and had to use a bunch of frequent flyer miles, so he invited me to go along for free. Wasn't that sweet of him?"

"Jimmi's always playing arm decoration to that guy but I don't like him. She could do better."

Jimmi was ready with a comeback, but I changed the subject. "Since you are going up to surprise your aunt, could I get a ride? My car is sitting over there with a flat tire."

Again in unison, they replied, "No problem, we rented a big cart to carry the surprise. You can ride up with us."

"I think we're going to get on famously." Jimmi added, "But enough about us, tell us about yourself."

I filled them in on my circumstances. But when they asked about my love life, I evaded most of their questions until Jimmi said, "I guess you don't have a boyfriend out here."

"Well, not yet. I've only been here a few days and I've been busy getting organized."

Jonnie held up one perfectly manicured finger, "Pardon us for a moment." She whispered in her sister's ear. Jimmi giggled and whispered a reply before they both turned and sat up straight with their hands on their knees. "We know someone who we think might interest you. If you aren't busy for lunch today, we could arrange a little get together at our aunt's. Are you up for it?"

I looked at them suspiciously. I may be young but I know a setup when I see it. Since the pickings seem a bit slim out here I replied, "I'd love to meet this mysterious person. By the way, have you ever heard the rumor that there are flying fish out here?"

"That's not a rumor," was their reply in unison. "We're world famous for our flying fish. What do you think of them?"

"Well, I haven't actually seen one yet."

Chapter Six

Dimple ran out to greet us, "My two lovelies." The girls ran into her arms and did a little dance together. I waited in the cart holding the oddly shaped package. Watching them made me miss my Mom. She'd hug Jojo tightly whenever we returned from an outing.

The twins carefully lifted their gift out of the cart. After they made me promise to be back for lunch at one, I walked back to my place. Veronica and the little ones were gone so the house was absolutely quiet.

At exactly one p.m. I rang Dimple's doorbell and waited. Soon she appeared from around the side of the house with an arm full of vegetables.

"Yoo Hoo! Hello Maddie."

"Hi Dimple, can Jimmi and Jonnie come out and play?" I asked in a little girl's voice.

"Oh, don't be a silly goose." She gave me a hug around my neck. "They drove their cart down to town an hour or so ago. Something about a surprise for you. Isn't that exciting?" She gushed, "I wonder what it could be."

Suddenly I wondered if I made a mistake coming to meet someone.

"At any rate, I'm sure it will be a surprise. Come, help me chop these veggies and tell me how you're getting settled in."

"I am concerned about the cost of keeping that big place running and the lawyer suggested I lease out some of the land for a cell phone tower."

"Ow!" Dimple dropped the knife. "I cut my finger."

She wrapped her hand in a towel and looked at me. "Is that really necessary? I mean - a cell phone tower out here? Don't those things give off radiation?"

"Why is everyone so against it? It's my property!"

Dimple put a bandage on her cut and changed the subject to the weather. I guess she knew I didn't want to talk about the tower.

"Yoo hoo!" There was that stereo sound again. The twins and a smiling Luke Garrett popped their heads in the doorway.

"You bad boy," Dimple chastened, "I hardly ever see you." She wiped her hands on her apron, gave him a big hug and shooed us out of the kitchen.

"I'll finish putting lunch together. You girls please set the porch table for lunch," she shot a knowing glance my way, "after you've introduced your guests to one another."

In unison, Jimmi and Jonnie said, "Maddie, we'd like you to meet..."

I finished their sentence, "Luke Garrett."

"Hey Maddie. Good to see you again, and so soon."

"Oopsie." Jimmi commented. "I guess you two have already met. Oh well, I should have expected that Luke would have already set his sights on you."

"We've only been out a couple of times." He assured them.

The twins followed me, dragging Luke along with them, "A couple of times? Wow. She's been here less than a week." Jonnie scolded, "We know you Luke, but Maddie, we just met today and she's really sweet. How'd you do that?"

"I helped her with some big problems since she's been here, and things have been all right I guess."

Jimmi turned to her sister, "We see all, we know all. We are after all, the Outhouse Sisters, but we must be slipping." They looked at us, "Now spill it."

At that moment Dimple handed him a big platter of corned beef sandwiches and a bowl of potato salad, and sat him down in a chair. She handed me a large jar of whole kosher dill pickles and sat me across from him. "Maddie," Jonnie leaned over to me, "Since you two have been out together, you should realize that we know Luke better than anyone. We're here to make sure he treats you right." She put her arm around my shoulder, "We girls have to stick together."

Luke swallowed hard, and took a drink from the glass of fresh lemonade Dimple had just placed in front of him.

Jonnie took a deep breath and spread her arms wide, "Isn't this a beautiful day?"

Jimmi passed the tray of sandwiches to me, "So how did you two meet?"

Luke answered, "She ran out in front of my truck."

"I did not. You were speeding down the road."

"You stood right in the middle of the street and..."

Dimple interrupted, "Please pass the potato salad."

"I did not..." I mumbled under my breath.

Luke whispered across the table to me. "I thought we had a wonderful time at lunch in the cave yesterday."

"You thought? Did you think before you lectured me about what I should or shouldn't do on my own property?"

"Is that what this is all about?" Luke's eyes widened.

"You just won't let it go." I shot back.

Everyone at the table stared at me in silence, mouths open, chewing arrested in mid-chew. Then I realized I was on my feet. The women spontaneously broke into applause. Slowly, I shrank down into my chair and in my tiniest voice, said, "I'm sorry but that's how I feel." I looked up from my sandwich knowing Luke would've left if he could, but the twins drove him here and he had no means of escape.

"Well, that's how it is." Luke interjected, "Don't I have a right to my opinion too?"

"Booo." Jonnie hissed.

"I see," he continued, "We have a double standard here. Maddie can build whatever she wants, but I can't express an opinion about it."

"Everyone is welcome to their opinion, but you are hardly being a good islander with this behavior toward our newest resident." Dimple added."

I could see he felt outnumbered and outgendered.

"Okay, okay, I won't be so verbal about my thoughts, but Maddie should consider the consequences of whatever she decides to do." He looked directly at me.

I replied, "I'll give you one more chance Luke. Show me that you can be more open-minded and I might change my opinion of you."

"Sister." Jonnie whispered to Jimmi, "Do you realize we are witnessing history in the making? Luke Garrett backed down to a woman."

"None of our friends will ever believe this." Jimmi replied.

"Don't you dare..." Luke said to the twins. "Just keep this between us."

"I don't know..." Jonnie cautioned, "If you keep your word, there's nothing to worry about."

I could see there was history between Luke and the Outhouse sisters, and now seemed as good a time as any to learn the truth about this guy.

Jonnie tugged on my arm, "Let's go for a walk." Jimmi echoed her sister and pulled Luke along.

"Don't stay out too long." Dimple called as she cleared our plates of half-eaten lunch, "I've still got dessert."

The three of us strolled arm in arm down the gravel path, with Luke following a few paces behind. Jimmi glanced back at him and said, "Did he tell you about his mother?" I shook my head.

Jonnie chimed in," Well, did he, at least, tell you what happened?"

"No."

"Do you two have to do this now?"

"Luke." Jimmi scolded, "It's been almost ten years..."

She pressed her forehead close to mine and whispered, "The truth is..."

"Oh God." Luke moaned, "Here we go. I'm going back to the house and lie down."

Jimmi stuck her tongue out at him, then turned to me and started again, "The truth, Maddie, is you would have loved his late mother."

"His late mother?"

Jonnie added, "It was the Loma Prieta earthquake. She was inside a store when the quake hit and got crushed by an iron support beam. That building was built by the company where Luke's father was a partner. Apparently, the firm cut corners, used substandard materials, bribed building inspectors and falsified test results. The senior partner went to prison, and his father had to sell the business. They lost everything."

"That's awful. So, his father has been a single dad and Luke hasn't had a mother?"

"It wasn't his fault, but his father felt responsible for her death - and for a long time that drove a wedge between Luke and him."

Jonnie added, "But... even though his father designed the buildings, it was his partner who was in charge of the construction and bought cheap, substandard materials. At least now his father is trying to do something to build a relationship with Luke, but they still have a long way to go."

"I had no idea. That's so sad."

We got back to the house and found Luke stretched out on the sofa with his shoes off. We took seats around the room.

Without opening his eyes, Luke asked, "So, Maddie, did you learn all the sad details of my childhood?"

I studied the figure lying on the sofa. He never let on that he had such a tragic history. "Enough for now." I answered, "Why? Is there more I should know?"

Jimmi jumped in, "Tons and tons..."

"We're just getting warmed up." Jonnie added.

Luke opened his eyes and looked at the twins, "Why don't we talk about it later. By the way, where are the guys - Bryce and what's his name?"

"Golf," they replied in unison. Jimmi said. "Bryce told me to remind you that you still owe him two-fifty from the last time you played."

Luke rolled off the sofa, "You know what, I think I'll take Maddie for a little walk and tell her my side of things."

In the dining room Jonnie and Jimmi had mixed themselves a couple of Martinis. With a knowing look to her sister, Jimmi said, "We're going to stay here and nurse these wonderful little drinks."

I looked back at the twins. They motioned for me to go.

When we were out of sight of the house, Luke stopped. "Maddie, I don't want you to feel pity because of what Jimmi and Jonnie told you. I've come to terms with my mother's death. My father wants her to have peace so he can move on. That way I can move on with my life too and that's the reason I choose not to talk about it."

"I can respect that, Luke. I'm sure Jimmi and Jonnie didn't mean any disrespect, they seem like really good friends and they obviously care about you."

He jammed his hands in his pockets.

As we neared the stable he looked around, "I meant to ask what with all the digging? Are you planting an orchard or something?" He pointed to all the freshly dug holes scattered around the area. "They look like they were made by giant gophers."

"No. It's really weird. These holes just appear, like those crop circles you read about in the tabloids. I guess I better check out the pasture later and see if there are any holes over there. One of the horses could get hurt if they stepped in one." We went into the stable, Javier was out and Fred was gone. He must have taken him for exercise.

"Luke, I lost both my parents... I think I can understand what you've been going through."

The muscles in his neck strained to hold back any emotion that might spill out. I placed my hands on his chest. He let his eyes drift down and held my hand. In contrast to his, my hands were tiny. Silently, in the grove of trees, we listened to the breeze in the branches and to our heartbeats, sharing something deep and personal.

Luke moved closer but I pulled away.

He glanced at his watch, "We should get back before the twins start thinking up stories about us."

On our walk back up the path I thought of how the truth of Luke's past helped him to show a softer side of himself I hadn't seen before. I held his arm, "Careful you don't step into one of those holes."

When we got back to Dimple's house, we heard laughter coming from inside.

"While you were out, Jimmi and Jonnie entertained me with their fantastic travel stories. Now that I know the secret life of that gawd awful African cat statue, she's just going to have to stay right where she is, unless, of course, I want the curse of Mubutu on my home."

"Dimple," Luke interrupted, "Thanks for the great lunch. I gotta to get back to work. Could you girls give me a ride back to town?"

"I'll give you a ride." Jimmi popped up, drunk, then slumped back into her seat next to Jonnie.

"Maddie, could you?" He nodded toward the two wasted redheads. "I don't want to cause any problems."

"Sure, why not?" I looked back at Dimple as we went out the front door. She gave me a little wink and closed the door behind us.

"I should have known better than to let those two kidnap me." Luke confided. "It's been so long since I last saw them, I forgot about their fondness for mixed drinks. By the way, the foundation of your building is in need of work. You should get that fixed before you open it to the public."

"Gee, you sound like a true real estate developer."

"You could pull some help together to finance your bed and breakfast instead of putting up a cell tower ..."

"Don't press your luck."

When we got back to Catalina Disposal Luke handed me a big plastic shopping bag. "Here, I bought some clothes for Veronica's kids. Will you give them to her?"

"Luke Garrett, don't tell me you're after that poor woman. The kids are adorable, but aren't you kind of young for a ready-made family?"

"That's mean, Maddie, very cruel. You don't know me. You may think you do, but you really don't."

I climbed back in the cart and drove back to Dimple's. After I parked it out front, I threw the bag of clothes over my shoulder and walked home. Silence usually helped me clear my head but it just made me angrier. When I sat down to write, I couldn't focus, so I got up and stood by the French doors. Maybe I could use a walk to calm down.

The grass was swaying with the breeze and as I walked I let myself go with the flow. Before long I found myself back at the stable. When I walked in, Javier was busy cleaning.

"Oh, *Señorita* Maddie - you scare me!"

"I'd like to take Lucy for a ride. Could you please saddle her up?"

"Sure *Señorita*."

I waited outside feeling the breeze on my face and the warmth of the sun. Javier helped me onto Lucy and I took off. I ran her hard, watching her mane flow with the wind until I could feel her breathing heavily. We galloped past the trees, scaring a few birds from their branches. I was on top of the world until Lucy took a misstep, reared back and bucked me off. I went flying over her head and landed on a sandy patch near the cliffs. Dazed, I checked to see if I broke anything before trying to move or stand. My left shoulder was sore and I'm sure there was going to be a big bruise on my butt. I looked back at Lucy to see if she was okay. She was trembling and licking at her left foreleg. Slowly I walked up and rubbed the side of her neck to calm her while I looked at her leg. She was bleeding! The cause was right there. She'd stepped in one of those stupid holes! There was no one to help us. Below the cliff I noticed a small sailboat moored near the cave. I looked up and down the beach but couldn't see anyone. Must be one of the surfers, but what would a surfer need with a sailboat?

I slowly led Lucy, limping, back to the stables and hoped she wasn't hurt too bad. Javier saw us and came running. "Ay Maddie! Oh Lucy...*¿Qué pasó?* What Happened?»

Lucy whinnied and lifted her foreleg to keep the weight off. Javier caressed her injured leg. "We were having a great time until she stepped into one of those holes."

He looked up at me, «This is not so very good. I call the *veterinario*."

I couldn't hold back my tears. Lucy was hurt pretty bad and there was nothing I could do but wait for the vet.

"Please go back to the house *Señorita* Maddie. I take care of this."

"Javier - you call me as soon as the vet arrives, okay?" Without looking up at me, he said, "*Sí, sí, por favor* you go now."

I ran crying back to the house. The Wagoneer was back and I saw Dimple standing in the door. "About time you showed up. Veronica called me, all worried. She called Luke and he said you left his office hours ago."

I told them what happened to Lucy. "It was all my fault Veronica! I shouldn't have run her so hard past those trees. She couldn't have seen the hole."

"You should call the sheriff," Dimple insisted, "Have them investigate. This is getting dangerous. Somebody is obviously sneaking up here and digging around."

"For what?" I cried. "What would they be digging for?"

"Well," Dimple replied, "I'm calling them right now. I know these boys. They'll help us figure this out."

In less than half an hour, the sheriff's four-wheel drive appeared, followed closely by the vet's truck.

The deputy's haircuts were identical and they wore identical sunglasses.

"Afternoon Miss. I'm Deputy Lopez and this is Deputy Malloy."

"I'll stay here with my kids." Veronica waved to us as Dimple and I rode with the deputies to the stable. The vet examined Lucy while the deputies asked Javier, "What do you know about these holes?"

"*No Diputado*, I find them for a couple of weeks now, more and more each day. Something is not good. I see a boat on the shore a few days before *Señorita* Maddie come to Dove Acres."

After an hour of checking out all the holes and searching up and down the cliff, they reported back.

"It doesn't make sense, why anyone would dig holes like that, and they're definitely man made. Unless..."

"Unless what? Do you know something?"

"We found these by the bottom of the cliff," the other deputy held up two rusty shovels and a rake.

"Now I am only speculating, but sometimes pot growers plant their crop in secluded spots with easy access. Now this is only a possibility." He made a few notes without looking up, "If I were you, I'd have a closed circuit surveillance system put in immediately." I told him about the sailboat I spotted below the cliffs. They said they'd look into it.

The vet appeared from the stable shaking her head. Javier rushed to her. "What? Is Lucy okay?"

"It's not good. Her leg is fractured. We can try to splint her leg and see if she heals, but Lucy is pretty old. I'm afraid we may have to put her down if she doesn't get better within a few weeks."

"Put her down?" I cried. "No! We'll take care of you girl. I'm so sorry. I did this to you, it's my fault."

Javier made the sign of the cross. He put his weathered arm on my shoulder and patted Lucy on the nose. "Not to worry *Señorita. Ay Dio.* I take good care of her."

The vet handed Javier a bottle of antibiotics, "Give her two of these in her feed every day for two weeks. Absolutely no riding until I say so. Rub her down with liniment and keep her cast dry. I'll check back."

The Vet drove off in a cloud of dust.

"Javier," I took his hand. "After you get Lucy settled, please come up to the house for supper."

"*Oh no, Señorita, grácias...*"

Dimple insisted, "*A las siete* Javier, at seven *por favor.*"

"How about you deputies?" She asked as we climbed back into the Sheriff's truck for the ride back to the house.

"Thanks, but we have to get back to town."

Chapter Seven

Somewhere in the bottom of my dresser drawer, a pair of very unglamorous, pink sweat pants and an oversized 'Hello Kitty' t-shirt were waiting to be found. This morning they decided not to cooperate. But after I found them, I jammed my clogs under my arm and quietly tiptoed downstairs and out the door without waking up Veronica or the kids.

"C'mon in." Dimple chimed, "What have you got there?"

"It's a shoe box with the Tiffany's brooch and a bunch of other pieces I told you about."

"Well, let's go into the dining room and you can show me what you found."

She pulled a chair over and sat next to me.

"Let's see what's in here." She opened the box and emptied the contents on a place mat.

"Where is the brooch?"

"It's... I thought it was in there." After frantically sifting through all the pieces I put my head in my hands, "Oh crap. I'll bet I dropped it after he... I mean, when I tried to climb out of the dumpster."

"You better get back there and get it before Luke processes all that trash."

"Sorry Dimple, I won't be gone long."

"That's okay, I'll look over the rest of these while you are gone... Drive carefully."

I rushed back to Catalina disposal and ran to the office. His father came out to greet me.

"Is Luke here?"

"Nope, sorry Maddie, he's out on a trash run. Is there something I can do for you?"

"Is there anyway you can reach him?"

He picked up a mobile radio from the counter. "Luke, this is dispatch, over."

"Luke here, what's up Dad? Over."

"I have an important message for you, over." Mr. Garrett handed me the radio. "Just push this red button when you want to talk and let go when you're finished so he can answer." He stood back and folded his arms.

"Luke, this is Maddie." There was no answer.

Mr. Garrett said, "Say over and let go of the red button."

"Oh, over."

"...addie? What're you doing there, over?"

"After all that searching, I think I dropped that brooch when I climbed out of the dumpster the other day. I'll have to climb back in and find it... over." I let go of the red button and looked at his father. He gave me a thumbs up.

"Oh gee, that's too bad," Luke replied, "I'm afraid it's not there anymore, so climbing back in the dumpster won't help, over."

"WHAT? Oh no! That was worth a fortune. What am I gonna do? Luke? Luke?" His father pried my finger off the red button.

"What you should do," Luke replied, "is chill. I have the brooch in my shirt pocket. I saw it fall out of your coveralls so I picked it up, over."

"You had it all this time and worried me sick? You are so mean..." Mr. Garrett pointed at my finger. "I mean, Over."

"I'll return it when I see you on Friday. Over."

"Friday?" I said into the radio. "What's Friday? Over."

"You can make a nice dinner for me in return for rescuing your jewelry, over"

"Wait, I..."

Mr. Garrett Sr. took the radio. "Luke, that's enough fooling around, what's your ten-twenty? over." Luke spoke back to his father in some kind of radio code, so I just waved and went back to Dimple's house. I was relieved the brooch was safe but I'll feel even better when I have it in my hands.

Dimple was still looking over the contents of the shoebox when I walked in. "Do you mind if I hang onto this box for a couple days? There are so many memories of your aunt and uncle in here. I just want to look at them and remember."

"Sure. I've got more back at the house. You're welcome to come over and go through some of it with me and you can keep any pictures that are special to you."

"You are sweet," Dimple gave me a kiss on the cheek before I went back home.

"You're sure up early," Veronica whispered.

"Oh Veronica, I have a big problem."

"Shhh. The children are still sleeping. I've made a healthy breakfast. I don't want you polluting yourself with all that microwaved fake food any longer."

"That's exactly why I need to talk to you." Scrunching up my hair and dreading the fact that I had to ask – no beg Veronica to teach me to cook. Not that I have anything against her, I just don't like to cook... especially for Luke Garrett.

"For goodness sakes, cheer up. It's a beautiful morning. Sit down and tell me about it."

After I described all the drama surrounding the lost brooch, Veronica asked, "Well, what do you want to make for him? It's your choice."

"Maybe you should choose - I'm clueless."

"Okay, it's a little cool at night so let's start with soup, chicken for the entree and we'll finish up with a simple dessert."

"Really Veronica? Do I look like Martha Stewart? I've never cooked anything more complicated than Ramen soup."

"Didn't you learn anything in Home Economics?"

"In what?"

"Oh never mind, they probably don't teach that anymore."

She opened her cookbooks, laid them open on the counter and away we went. The downside was that our fun morning turned into "Cooking for Dummies." Veronica was so patient and showed me lots of shortcuts to make things easier for me, but I don't know if she'll ever let me in her kitchen again.

"Okay," she proclaimed, "you're all set for Luke."

"Thanks for your help." I gave her a hug, "I have to go pick up my Mustang from the mechanic."

I took the list of ingredients Veronica made for me to Pinkie's Market. She loaded me up with several bags of food and frozen stuff that I lugged back to my kitchen. All the frozen stuff went in the freezer and I stuffed the raw veggies in the refrigerator. I took a deep breath and looked around the room until panic set in. So, exposing myself as the scared cooking newbie, I was. I called Veronica's cell. "Help!"

She had taken the kids to free day camp in town and was at the bank.

"Maddie, don't touch anything until I get there."

I hung up and slumped onto a chair, "I should be able to do this. It's cooking, not brain surgery and I've had a year of college."

When the cavalry arrived, Veronica peered into the kitchen door where I was staring blankly at the food piled on the counter.

After a couple of hours Veronica put her arm around my shoulder and said, "See how easy that was? Let's go have a cup of tea."

I was still scribbling the last of the instructions, while Veronica sat back and took a sip from her cup.

"You should have no trouble on Friday when you do this for real." She untied her apron, slurped last drop from her cup and headed for the door, "I gotta get back to town - things to do."

"You'll be here if I need it, right?"

She shook her head, "This is your thing. You need to do it." She sounded like the big sister I never had.

I made sure she had left, I called Jojo at the campground.

"What's the matter kiddo? Luke again?"

"No, I need some cooking advice."

"Madeline van der Wald cooking? Oh... Don't make me laugh, come on, Maddie what's the matter - really."

"Sometimes you can be really mean JoJo. I'm not kidding, Luke thinks I'm going to make a home cooked dinner for him Friday night. Veronica already tried to teach me, but I'm just not getting this."

"Good thing you're starting now, because there is a learning curve to this. I mean it's more that pushing the button marked "Frozen Entree" on the microwave."

"Stop teasing me. I bought all the stuff Veronica told me to get. She even tried to show me how to make it all this morning...but I can't. I don't know what's wrong with me. I just know it's going to be a disaster."

"Okay," JoJo asked, "What's on the menu?"

I got out the paper and read, "French onion soup, Coq au Vin, with mushrooms and green beans, and..." I flipped through the pages, "...Raspberry Trifle for dessert."

"Wow. You know what I do? I have a secret weapon."

"Oh, you know a good caterer here?"

"Uh...No, but I get this magazine called Real Simple, it's the Anti-Martha Stewart way of doing things. Let me look them up tonight when I get home. I'll email the recipes and call you tomorrow. If I can make this stuff, I'm sure you can... gotta go, bye." I felt a little better, but not much.

On Friday Luke arrived at precisely six-thirty p.m. with a bottle of wine under his arm. I opened the door and without smiling, invited him inside.

"Do you have it?" I asked.

"Did you cook for me?"

"First, let me see it."

"Not until after we eat. We had a deal....remember?"

"I remember."

"Can I ask you something?" he said, holding back the urge to laugh. "Why are we talking like spies?"

"I don't know." I giggled, "Silly, isn't it."

While I put the bottle of wine to chill, Luke browsed around the living room scrutinizing all the photos on the wall of Aunt Helen and George taken with famous people.

"Make yourself comfortable, I just need to finish up a couple little things in the kitchen."

Luke wandered over to the French doors and stepped outside onto the patio. I saw him through the doorway looking out at the ocean and wondered what he was thinking.

When I announced, "Dinner's ready," he walked into the dining room, "This is a truly beautiful location. There aren't many places left in California like this. My father says he hopes you realize what a treasure you have here."

"Since I got here, I've been learning to appreciate what my aunt has done for me."

He followed me to the table and pulled my chair out for me.

"We're starting with French onion soup." I explained and shared a basket of sourdough bread. We ate quietly, without making much eye contact. After I nervously cleared the bowls from the left side, I brought out the baked chicken ala JoJo and refilled our glasses, "You seem to think you know a lot about me, Luke, but there's a lot more to me than meets the eye."

He made sort of a "hmmph" sound and coughed, almost choking on his food, and took a swallow of water. "...and," I continued, "I know practically nothing about you."

Clearing his throat, he said, "What do you want to know about me that Jimmi and Jonnie didn't tell you. I mean they practically read my whole personal file to you."

"I mean other stuff."

"Well, I'm six foot two inches tall. Do I have any brothers or sisters?...no. Do I need glasses to drive?... no. What made me decide to get into the waste management business?... It's very profitable, everyone makes garbage."

"I didn't mean to make it sound like an interrogation, but I'm going to be living on this island for at least six months and I felt we could get to know each other better. I thought, maybe we could be friends. I guess I was wrong."

I raised my eyes to gauge his reaction. To my surprise, he looked totally ashamed, but I wasn't going to let him pull the hurt puppy routine on me.

"I'm sorry Maddie, please go on."

"Take the way we met... I don't believe in random occurrences... do you?"

I realized that I had just asked an awfully deep question for such a casual dinner, but the words were out there now and all I could do was sit back and watch them ricochet off of his head and fall to the floor. But that didn't happen. Instead, Luke responded in a most unexpected manner,

"I have to admit... I feel the same way. It's as if each experience in our lives, whether positive or negative, prepares us for something in the future." He explained, "That day at the boat landing... if we hadn't met that day, chances are, we wouldn't be sitting here together right now."

I was lost in his steel gray eyes when he answered my question in such an unexpected way.

"And because," I responded, "I accidentally threw my aunt's brooch out with the trash. By the way, I'm really grateful you found it."

"You're welcome." He raised his glass to me.

What? You're welcome? Is that it? I fulfilled my end of the bargain. I cooked his stupid dinner. Don't I get any points for the food or the time I spent making myself look presentable for him?

"I'll be back in a second," and took our dirty dishes to the kitchen.

I came back two dessert dishes on a silver tray. Carefully, I placed one in front of Luke and the other at my spot.

"Is this what I think it is?" Luke asked, trying to be as noncritical as possible, "One of those little Twinkie things?"

A scoop of vanilla ice cream sat in the center of his dish and what appeared to him to be a Twinkie, drizzled with chocolate sauce and topped with crushed macadamia nuts and fresh raspberries. I corrected him, "It's a Lady Finger."

He picked up his dish and eyed it suspiciously, turning it around to examine every side. "I smell rum."

"It's a Lady Finger." I reiterated as I watched him set the dish down.

"Just taste it, please."

Luke picked up the properly chilled fork and sampled a small piece.

"Mmm. Wow, Maddie. This is delicious. I guess looks can be deceiving."

"Now there's something else I've learned about you Luke. You like sweet things with a little kick in them... even if you think it's just a Twinkie. Dimple gave me some rum for it."

My improvised dessert appeared to be a hit. All that coaching from Dimple, Veronica and JoJo gave me enough confidence to try using things I had on hand.

After we finished, I seized the opportunity to ask, "Now may I have my brooch?"

"Sure thing, you've kept your part of the deal with an excellent dinner. But... I would like to pin it on you, if you don't mind. That way you won't drop it before I leave."

First I sneered and stuck out my tongue, then I pointed to a spot on my collar where he could pin it. He reached into his shirt pocket and held it between his thumb and forefinger. He must have cleaned and polished it because it sparkled like it had just come out of the display case.

He pushed his chair out and came over to me, I held my breath. He was careful not to ruin my blouse as he fumbled with the pinback. He was so very close I could feel goosebumps going up my spine and my legs beginning to weaken. Good thing I was sitting down. It took me a moment before I remembered to start breathing again.

He finally fastened it, "This pin looks great on you." and looked into my eyes, "I think you're kind of pretty."

Kind of? After what I went through for this guy?

"You really think so?" I batted my eyelashes at him. "I mean seriously, you really like how it looks on me?" He stood back to admire both me and the pin.

"Definitely."

As I brushed my hair back away from my shoulder so he could see the pin better I felt myself blush. I had to summon all my strength to keep from kissing him like I did in the dumpster.

"Yes, very pretty, I like it." he said.

This evening was going a lot better than I expected. He kept his word and I still had those goosebumps.

Chapter Eight

First thing in the morning I picked up a message from Jojo. Just hearing her say she'd been on the mainland and was coming back today made me yearn for the freeways and the fast pace I left behind for Catalina, but the sweet aroma of buttery croissants distracted me. Veronica had baked a batch for breakfast.

Jojo showed up just as they were cooling on the kitchen counter. Veronica wrapped up a couple for her kids and took them to day camp. While Jojo downed two more croissants with her coffee, I told her about the financial issues.

"I have to do something soon or we might lose this place. Right now, renting a spot for a cell phone tower seems the fastest way to generate income." Jojo listened intently and sipped her third cup of coffee. "I'm telling you this because half of this property belongs to you and I'd like your input before I make a decision. Whether you were in the will or not, you're a partner in this."

"Stop right there." she held up her hand and looked me straight in the eye. "First of all, I'm not your blood relative."

"How could you say that? Mom and Dad adopted you. Legally you're my sister and entitled to half this inheritance."

She waited a long time to speak, "They never adopted me - legally."

My throat tightened, "But they raised us as sisters and I always thought it was legal."

"They were my legal guardians, but I learned just before they died that they never adopted me. I brought this to their attention and YOUR father said to me, "You're not a real Van der Wald, and I'm not going to cheat my flesh and blood daughter out of half her inheritance."

The deep hurt and betrayal brought tears to her eyes. "I'd always thought they loved me as much as they loved you, but when your father said that, I knew it wasn't true. He never considered me part of the family. I was just a charity case to him."

"That makes no sense Jojo. They showed us the same love and affection. We got the same education. We were in scouts and basketball together. They even gave us the exact dresses for prom night, different colors, but they were the same."

Jojo put her face in her hands and sobbed, "They never gave me their name, never made me a real member of the family. When your father said that to me, I felt like he slammed a door in my face. I was nothing, nobody."

I reached for her hand but she pulled back.

"After I moved away I researched my roots and found out I'm part Tongva, but that's all. My ancestors inhabited this island centuries ago. That's why I live here now. It's my ancestral home - my land. Your father took away my family and I didn't fit in to your world. My true history had been hidden from me. I was nobody until I found my people."

"But Jojo, Mother loved you like her own, she doted over both of us at school and...everywhere. How could you say that?"

"I know, I owe them a lot... my health, education, the stuff they bought me and the love they showed. But when I learned I was never accepted into what I thought was my own family, I felt like I had only been looking through a window at a family gathered around a warm fireplace and I was outside in a storm."

"Is that why you left after the funeral and never returned my calls?"

"I thought that was the way they wanted it. I did my job by acting the part of your sister. Once we grew up, I knew my presence was not needed or wanted."

"They said that?"

"Not in so many words, but that's how it made me feel."

"I can't believe that. Our parents weren't like that. Jojo, you are my family, my only family. Whatever happened between my parents and you is in past. It's us now, you and me. It will always be that way. You're my sister and I love you."

She shook her head. "If you mean what you say, then don't put the cell phone tower on this land. This is Tongva land, holy and sacred mother earth. You can't desecrate it with commercial structures."

"...and my bed and breakfast idea, are you against that too?"

"The land was here since before man came. The white man built on top of it and covered over much of my people's history, but none of that matters now. This is your home now. Please don't ruin it like the white man did in Hawaii."

"What am I supposed to do? How will I pay for the expenses of running this place? Even as it is, my inheritance will be gone in less than a year then I have nothing."

"Ever hear of getting a job, Maddie? It might do you some good to learn what the real world is like instead of feeling sorry for yourself."

"But I can't go anywhere for six months and I can't make enough money with a job on the island. A bed and breakfast inn will bring people here to enjoy the breathtaking views, and if we plan it right, the environment won't be disturbed. Have you even seen the rest of this place?" She shook her head. "Well, it's huge. Let's go for a horseback ride and I'll introduce you to OUR land."

We walked to the stables where she asked, "What happened to that one?" pointing to Lucy. I found it hard to tell her how Lucy got injured by one of those damn holes.

I introduced her to Javier and asked him to saddle up Ethel and Ricky.

"I don't need a saddle" Jojo said, "I'll ride bareback!"

"Are you serious?"

"Sure, I learned to do this at a reservation one weekend." We trotted for a few minutes as I pointed out the boundaries of the property.

"Be careful of those holes - Please!"

She gave me a deadpan stare. "First promise me there'll be no cell towers or fancy development on my land." Before I could respond, she gave Ricky a sharp swat on the rump with the palm of her hand and took off at a full gallop. I had to push Ethel hard to catch her. I wanted to tell her I was going to get her name added to the deed, but she looked so happy riding Ricky with the wind blowing her hair. She stopped near the cliffs and patted the horse on the neck while he panted heavily. I slowed up and trotted to her side. "Well?" I asked, "What do you think of it?"

She smiled at me, "It's so much bigger that I'd imagined and I'm glad so much of it is untouched - well, except for all those holes. Those are dangerous. Is that what happened to Lucy? Why are they there? What are they for?"

"Frankly, I have no idea how they got there. Javier and I aren't doing any digging. After Lucy's accident, the Sheriffs came up and investigated. It must be trespassers or something."

Back at the house, I poured some lemonade for us and flopped in the living room. Jojo noticed the shells I brought back from the cave.

"I still have some paperwork to do in order to get you on the deed, Jojo. It probably won't happen until this six months is up."

"Right, six months, huh?"

"Trust me Jojo, you're my only sister. You always have been and always will be."

"Historically, maybe yes, in name and in my mind - no. I guess I'm supposed to feel like I owe your parents and you. We were sisters but I felt more like your shadow. So until I find my blood family, if that ever happens..."

She flipped her cell phone open and looked her messages, "I gotta go," and left without a goodbye or a hug. I felt empty and a bit guilty as I watched her drive away and wondered why my father would have said those terrible things to her.

I called Tom. Maybe I could get back to L.A. for a little while and see some of my friends. "Am I allowed to go back to the mainland at all during this time? Like for a weekend? Or vacation?"

"Only in the event of a medical emergency. Why?"

"All my friends and my life are back on the mainland and most of them can't afford to come over just to visit and do you realize this whole island rolls up at nine?"

"Tell you what, let me take you to dinner on the mainland tomorrow night. I know a nice place. It's a bit dressy if that's okay with you."

"Dressy? There's no place to go dressed up on this island."

"Be ready at five."

***

That evening Tom showed up with flowers but I wasn't expecting a date so much as a nice evening out with my attorney! Going out to dinner in a golf cart seemed a bit anticlimactic, but this is Catalina Island. What's a girl to do?

To my surprise he drove us to the helipad in Avalon where a helicopter was waiting with the engine running.

In a few minutes we landed on the roof of a hotel in Serena Beach and were escorted to the penthouse restaurant where a private party was being held

We made our way through the restaurant. All the while I was curious why Tom would plan such a fancy evening. We pushed past the crowd to a candlelit table near the window where we talked about my Aunt Helen and Dove Acres. He picked at his food for a while before reaching across and taking my hand. "I care for you very much Maddie."

"Whoa!" I pulled my hand away and put it in my lap.

He looked surprised, "I just wanted to say, I haven't spent much time thinking about a personal life. My father's law practice has kept me very busy, just as he planned it. My staff is the best but my work has taken over my life. I want to settle down."

I think my mouth was hanging open. He looked like he expected a response from me but I had no idea what to say. This was supposed to be a business arrangement.

"I certainly didn't plan to feel like this." Tom mumbled, "But from the first time I saw you..."

When he shifted in his seat, I thought for sure he was going to get down on his knee and propose!

"Look, Tom. I don't even know you. I mean, my Aunt Helen just died a few of weeks ago and I've only been on the island a short time."

"Sure, sweetheart, I can understand how you must feel, all alone and uncertain. I hoped by sharing my feelings it would help you to feel like you belong instead of being isolated on the estate."

"Wait – please don't call me Sweetheart. I'm a client. For now, just call me Maddie or Madeline." I was irritated, but I was determined to be polite. After all, he was my ride home. "Tom, you're very sweet and I appreciate this evening. You've helped me focus." I reached for both his hands, "Thank you, but I need time. I hope you understand."

He nodded looked down at his plate. After dessert we headed for the helipad. On our way out we passed a table where I saw two familiar faces.

"Jimmi and Jonnie Outhouse," I was surprised I recognized them. They were dressed in tiny little black cocktail dresses and had their hair done up like fashion models.

"Why Maddie, what a surprise! Bryce and his friend Stuart both stood to shake my hand, very old school. Bryce shook

Tom's hand but Stuart kept his distance and simply nodded when I introduced them. Tom on the other hand avoided all eye contact with Stuart and focused on the twins. Something was up between those two guys. I asked Tom about it on the way to the helicopter.

"Stuart and I go way back," was his only response and left it at that. I chose not to pursue it any further.

On the elevator up to the roof, he put his coat around my shoulders to shield me from the chill, "I know you haven't made up your mind yet, but I found a firm interested in the cell tower. You'll need to decide soon, their bid offer will not last forever and they are interested."

"Bid offer?"

"These companies usually have several sites in mind and the different landowners bid for the use of their land. "That's where you come in. You will need to meet with them and basically sell the advantages of your property."

"I've never done anything like that! I wouldn't know where to start!"

"I'll coach you, like I promised I would for your aunt. Funny - she used the exact words when I brought up the bidding process to her. It must run in your family."

"Excuse me? I'll have to research some of this on my own before I can make a decision like that."

On the drive back up to Dove Acres Tom looked at me, "I didn't mean to upset you Maddie. Take all the time you need. Just remember what I said."

I couldn't enjoy the full moon with Tom's constant talking. He talked about anything and everything except the cell tower, but I wasn't listening.

He stopped by my garage, turned off the cart and put his arm around me. "Listen, Maddie. I know you have a lot on your mind but please don't let it spoil our evening." He reached for my hand but I crossed my arms in front of me.

"I had a great evening with you, Ms. Maddie Van der Wald." He pushed the side of my hair back to kiss me, but I turned away.

"Please don't. Not now."

He put his hands in his pockets. "Well, get a good night's sleep. I'll call you when you're focused and we can discuss things further."

***

The next day I drove to town for my mail and to check into getting a closed circuit TV system and alarm. The only available parking spot was a block from the Post Office. Since I was near Pinkie's Market I stopped in to visit her. On the way back to my car, I saw a cell phone shop and plopped my phone down on the counter. "This thing doesn't work on the back side of the island. Do you have something that does?"

"Sure." He pulled a small box from under the counter, took out a phone and set it on the counter. It looked almost exactly like mine.

"So, what's the difference between that and the one I have?"

"The one you have is old school. It gets its signal from relay towers located all around the area, but there aren't any on the other side of the island, mostly because nobody lives there."

"FYI, I live over there."

"Oh, Sorry." He picked up the one he brought out, "This phone gets its signal from satellites orbiting above the earth. So you can be pretty much anywhere in the world and still get a connection."

"Whatever, just sign me up, please."

"I can have it tomorrow. This is just a demo model."

I started for the Post Office. Some weird bum was standing by the Post Office entrance, muttering to himself. I took a nervous glance at him as I passed by, but made sure not to make eye contact.

"Any mail for Madeline Van der Wald or Helen DeVine?"

The Postmaster looked over her glasses at me and asked, "You staying up at Dove Acres?"

I nodded.

"You must be Madeline." She smiled, "I'm sorry, but I'm still going to have to see some I.D." She eyed my driver's license, "And how are you adjusting to island life?" She asked, while she sorted through the mail, pulling out several envelopes.

"When I meet people like you," I read her name tag, "Martha, I know I'm going to enjoy my stay. By the way, there's a guy hanging around outside... do you know who he is?"

Martha lifted up the section of counter and looked out the door to see.

"Nope, don't know who he is. Every so often he asks if any mail has come marked General Delivery. He showed up about a month ago and mostly hangs out on the corner. The Sheriff and the Chamber of Commerce won't let that go on too long. It scares the tourists." She grinned broadly and said, "Speaking of tourists, how's your big plans coming along for Dove Acres. That should attract the tourists - how exciting."

"My big plans?"

"You know, the health spa, golf course... All that kinda stuff. It should work out really well - unless the ghost stories spook them."

I took the bundle of mail from her. Suddenly, I felt like I was in a movie where everyone knew the plot except me.

"Martha - Did you say ghost stories? I've never... you mean Dove Acres?"

"I don't know. Now that I think back, it was that guy outside. Yes, he came in here the other day begging for coffee money. He was mumbling something about Dove Acres being haunted and pirate gold, and Oh, jeez - he reeked like somethin' died."

"I know, he gives me the creeps too."

On the way back to my car, I looked through my mail until I walked right into someone. I looked up - Raylene blocked my path. Her legs were planted apart, arms folded in front of her with a scowl on her face.

"I know you've been seeing Luke." She snarled through clenched teeth. "He's mine."

I tucked the mail under my arm, "Who?"

"Like you don't know... Luke of course. Keep away from him if you don't want trouble."

"What?" I answered, "Raylene sweetie, you're underage and way too young for Luke. Finish high school before you hook up with a guy. You're going to get him in trouble."

"I don't care, bitch." She walked away, stopped and turned to face me. "Just stay away or you'll be sorry. It's a small island. Things happen." She spun back and threw her arm up and without looking at me, flipped me off.

This was all I needed, a teen drama queen with an attitude, then I realized she was only four years younger than me.

I stopped back by Pinkie's place to talk some sense into her. She was gone but Pinkie was there. "I guess Raylene found you, she left here all pissed off."

"What's with her and Luke, she's way too young to be chasing him."

"I know, but she's sixteen. Remember sixteen Maddie? Her hormones are running the show right now. I've been her foster mother for two years now and being here on the island keeps her out of more trouble than she would get into on the mainland."

"But I'm not really interested in Luke. We're friends, that's all. Could you please tell her that?"

Pinkie smiled and winked, "So, you really think you and Luke are just friends?"

"Of course, we have nothing at all in common. Believe me. And we're not even neighbors. He lives on a boat."

"Did Raylene, 'Or else', you?" Pinkie asked, "She can be a tough little snot, but I'll talk to her. And just so you know... Luke hasn't done anything to encourage her."

"Well, she got in my face and I don't appreciate it."

"In her defense - The poor child is desperate for a father figure."

I sighed and went back to my car. After the way my morning had been going I shouldn't have been surprised when I found "BITCH" scrawled on my windshield in red lipstick. I had a pretty good idea whose lipstick it was, and I wasn't going to take this from her. I drove over to Catalina Disposal, parked right in front of the office window and pressed the horn. Luke rushed outside and saw the scrawl on my windshield.

"You better talk to Raylene." I shouted, "This is getting out of hand. You need to do something."

Luke scratched his head, "Just a minute..." He ducked into the office and returned with a roll of paper towels and a spray bottle of glass cleaner. "I told her that who I see is none of her business." He mumbled aloud as he scrubbed the crimson "B" off my windshield. "But you have to admit she is hot. I mean drop-dead gorgeous."

"Luke! How can you even say that?"

"...and, of course way too young. C'mon Maddie. She's a kid! Where's your sense of humor?"

"Well, it's not funny. Do her parents know what's going on?"

While he scrubbed the "IT" off the glass he commented, "Yeah, her parents... that could be a problem. You see they're divorced, her dad's in jail for assault."

"What about her mom?"

He just shrugged after he wiped the "CH" off, "Who knows?" and sprayed some of the cleaner on his hands and wiped off the red stains. "I gotta get back to work, but I promise I'll talk to her."

Avalon, I've learned, is a small town. Even if it's only about thirty five miles from Los Angeles, but small town it is and news travels fast. I'm sure most of the people here saw the big red letters on my windshield.

I dropped the mail on the table when I got home, poured a glass of lemonade and went onto the patio where I closed my eyes and took in a big cleansing breath.

My eyes popped open when I heard Luke's truck coming up the road. What was I going to say?

"Hey," He began, "I was just talking to..."

"So what are you going to do about it?" I was firm with my arms crossed.

He stood there looking at me, "Well, I don't know, I thought I'd check to see if there is anything I could do."

"You wanted to check to see if there is anything you could do? Well that's stupid, it's your problem bleeding over onto me."

"How is this my problem?"

"Don't be self-righteous with me, Mr. Luke Garrett. I have nothing to do with it. I talked to Pinkie and she agrees it needs to be handled."

"Sure, it could be dangerous, especially since you're here alone with Veronica and the kids. It's not safe."

"So you'll do something about it?"

Confused he shook his head, "I can't. You need to call the Sheriff in order to figure out what to do."

"Why the Sheriff? Are you too chicken to face Raylene?"

"Raylene? What in God's name are you talking about?"

"Raylene! Who else? I don't like to be threatened and I certainly think Pinkie has a few ideas that could..."

"Hold it! Hold it! I was talking to Javier, he's worried about the holes he found over near the cliffs. I was concerned..."

"Didn't Pinkie talk to you about what Raylene said to me?"

"Well, yeah, but it's no big deal. There's nothing between us. Absolutely nothing."

I tried to be sympathetic to Raylene's situation and listened to what Luke had to say.

"She gushes all over my father too when he comes into the store. So, maybe she thinks of me as a big brother.

"Uh huh, big brother? Is that why you had lipstick all over you?"

"Okay, so maybe she's got a little crush on me."

"Well, what are we going to do about it?"

"We... aren't going to do anything, Maddie. I'm going to talk to her, and I'll set her straight. Are we clear on that?"

"Maybe Jojo knows someone from camp." I suggested, "I could hook her up with someone her own age and..."

"Maddie," Luke interrupted, "Don't get any ideas. Let me handle this. It's really my problem. Now... the real reason I came by... You have some trouble with trespassers. You should contact the sheriff and have them investigate it."

"I did already, the sheriff's deputies were up here a few days ago to check out the property... and I'm having an alarm system installed today."

"I can check on you throughout the day and tonight. That is, if you'd like me to."

"There's no need for that, but thanks for the offer. I gotta go Luke, the security guys should be here shortly."

"Maddie, before you go," he came closer to the door, "I want you to know I like you very much. I'll come by and check on you anyway."

"...and Raylene?"

"I'll take care of her in my own way."

"Just be sure you do. I don't want her in my face again."

"Oh, just so you know... I am the security guy. I install security systems on the island."

Wait - Did he say I like you very much? And what was that other thing - He's the security company too? What is this - Hooterville?

"I'll send one of my guys over this afternoon to give you an estimate."

Luke kept his word and stopped after supper to check on us. He even helped with the dishes. The little ones were playing on the floor with a bag of blocks Pinkie had given them when Nicholas asked, "Mommy, where is the light ghost?"

"Honey, there are no such things as ghosts it's just the light reflecting on the wall. Remember when we put our hand in front of it."

I seemed to recall a reflection shimmering on the wall yesterday morning.

"What do you think Luke, ghosts or no ghosts?"

He was examining the shells we found in the cave that I'd left on the end table. "These look like they were carved, I think."

Sarcastically, I commented, "Maybe the dancing ghosts carved them and put them in the cave."

He put them back. "Stranger things have happened."

"Nicholas honey, there's no such thing as ghosts." Veronica hugged him, "Those are only stories." But Nicholas wasn't convince so I did what my father did for me once.

"Look Nicholas." I shined a lamp at the wall and played shadow puppets. Luke did animals I never knew you could do with your fingers. He had the kids laughing and giggling in no time.

While the show went on, Veronica whispered to me, "Nicholas has been waking up with nightmares in the middle of the night... something about falling into holes in the wall. I don't know where he gets these things ideas."

Before he left, Luke assured me the alarm and security installation would be finished by the end of the day tomorrow and I'll have a knock-em-dead gate. All I saw was more money out of pocket.

After everyone else was in bed I leaned my hands on the edge of the bathroom sink and stared at myself in the mirror. "What are you going to do Maddie?" Nobody can help me. Was my trip here, a boat ride to Hell? I put my head down and watched my tears fall into the sink leaving little rivulets that ran down toward the drain.

Chapter Nine

"Jussaminnuh!" I mumbled into the phone, it wasn't even eight in the morning. "I huf a moufoo of cirrl!"

Chewing frantically, I swallowed hard and was finally able to say, "Sorry, I had a mouthful of cereal."

It was Jojo and she wanted to know how things went with Tom and the will. "He's calling me today. I'll let you know what happens. Okay?"

By lunchtime the fog had still not lifted and everything was dripping wet. I wished the sun would come out. Veronica was with the kids at preschool for a parent's orientation day. I sent a text to Jojo with my new satellite phone. It rocks! "No call yet C U later - M."

Tom finally called back, "Are you ready to talk business yet? This is very important. I emailed the info for our presentation to Cellcom today. You need to spend time going over this."

He was being way too bossy. So I decided to read up on all this and be ready for him tomorrow. Besides I was getting tired of being told you gotta do this and you gotta do that. I didn't like getting bullied.

"Just chill Mr. Silverman and keep in mind, this is my property not yours." I was sorry I said that as soon as the last word left my mouth.

He was quiet for a while, "I promised your aunt I'd help you and all I'm trying to..."

"Everyone prepares in different ways. I'll do my best. Cellcom is wrong if they think they're the only game in town." Actually, I was really nervous about speaking to a big corporation.

"If they want to use my land why can't they just contact me and we'll tell them what it's going to cost them. They can take it or leave it."

"Sweetheart, it doesn't work that way."

"Cellcom will make a lot of money by having this tower here and I need to make money from it too... and what did I say about calling me that?"

I pulled up his email on my computer and read where he'd highlighted the required area to the square foot.

"This is right on top of the spot where the stables are Tom. What about the horses?"

"We can have Cellcom move it or build another stable - a more modern stable."

I've never had to deal with this amount of money before. I thought of the changes I could make to the house, new stables, and maybe add a boat dock.

"Maddie," Tom lectured, "Remember to look each person in the eye and use the wording in the papers I emailed."

"I'm going to have to look up a lot of these words. I'm not a lawyer or accountant."

"Just memorize the text."

"Tom, I have no idea what I'm talking about. I need to use my own words or it just won't sound right." I read back some of the gobbledeegook he sent.

He let a big sigh into the phone, "Look Maddie, I know you're trying, but you're butchering it. Practice!"

"Are you kidding? You want me to memorize twenty-two points - twenty-two?"

"Look Sweetheart, use your own words, if you have to, but include all twenty-two points. They can be in any order, but they all have to be there."

"Tom? What did I say about calling me that?"

"Oh, my bad. Don't let them gang up on you. They may try the good cop/bad cop ploy, but just stick to the points."

"What if they ask me a question? What am I supposed to say?"

"I'll answer their questions. Just work on the presentation."

"How much time do we have?"

"I've scheduled a tour of the property today at one. I've reserved a conference room for our appointment at the bank tomorrow at three p.m."

"TOMORROW? " I shouted, "Are you crazy? You set this all up without asking me first?" I couldn't hear the rest of what he said. My head was pounding.

"I'm telling you now. Don't worry, we'll do fine. I mean, you'll do great. I'll call tomorr..."

I was so mad I hung up on him. If he was here I'd have thrown something at him, but I need the money. So what was I supposed to do? I made myself some tea and put together a study guide. It was how I studied for my finals and SAT tests. After I looked up some of the words, I changed some like reciprocity to exchange and draw-down to loss of income which made it easier to remember and more believable, besides, reciprocity was impossible to pronounce. My cell phone rang. When I looked at the clock, I discovered I'd been cramming for two hours straight.

It was Luke, "Hey, I thought I'd stop by. I have a surprise to show you.

I really needed a break. "I can only spend two hours, no more." I must've sounded bitchy but I was stressed. "Got it? 'cause I'm really busy."

Luke arrived in shorts and deck shoes. He wanted to go to Avalon. I insisted on driving so I could be sure and get back and finish preparing, and I sure wasn't going to tell him why. I don't think I said much on the way to town because I had words and numbers swirling in my head.

We stopped at a spot under a tree around the other side of the Casino, facing Descanso Beach for what he called it a "Round picnic." That's a pizza on a blanket. I took a deep breath, put on my sunglasses and looked out at the harbor. The noon sun gave everything a bright glow. "Is your boat out there?"

He counted over seven boats with his bread stick, stopping at a beautiful white sloop with teak decks and trim. "That's her right there."

"It's very pretty, could I go aboard some time?"

He swallowed a sip of beer and then another. I was glad that I was driving.

"I'd love to show her to you."

This was a comfortable date so far, no mention of the tower or my property. Finally something that Luke and I agreed on, though I'm not sure what it is was.

"If you want, we could go on board now. But you should know the flying fish only come out after dark, mostly."

"Well," I looked at my watch, "I don't have time for that today. I really need to get back soon."

"Well than I have another surprise for you." He packed up our trash like the good boy scout he was. He told me to drive to Catalina Disposal. Mr. Garrett Sr. opened the door and escorted me into his office where huge sheets of paper were laid out on a large conference table. As Luke passed him, he asked, "Luke. Have you been drinking?"

"Just a couple of beers, but don't worry. Maddie's driving."

His father made a throaty growling noise and shook his head, "We've put together some sketch ideas for Dove Acres."

Luke frowned at him, "I got this Dad." His father stood back. I crossed my arms.

"Now, these are just some brainstorming thoughts I was sharing with my father, but I'd like your opinion."

The older Mr. Garrett added, "I've never seen Luke as excited about a project before Maddie. He's put in a lot of late nights on this. Please take a look. Remember, nothing here is etched in stone."

"Yet." Luke added.

"Go ahead Luke, show her your ideas."

"Thanks Dad, don't you have some phone calls to make?"

His father whispered , "Don't push your luck with me son or her." As he went into the other room and closed the door. Luke pulled back the cover sheet. Before me appeared a most beautiful rendering of Dove Acres.

"It's a really beautiful drawing Luke." I was as tactful as I could be, "The house and grounds look the same."

He gave me an odd stare, " Good... That's what I was going for."

I obviously missed something. "You told me you wanted to show me some idea sketches."

"Aha. Check this out." With the flourish of a magician, he pulled a large packet from under the table. Unwrapping what looked like a large transparency, he placed it over the drawing. To my amazement, my aunt's house was transformed. What was a two story Monterey style building, became a very romantic looking hacienda, like something plucked from the hills of old Mexico. His design suggestions were all on the clear overlay. With the flick of the wrist I could lift it up and see where the changes were made.

"I love the flowered arbor leading from the drive to the main entrance... and the terra cotta pavers on the drive. Oh, and I love the shutters on all the windows... Luke, it's beautiful. What do you think the ocean side would look like?"

"Just relax, I took the whole thing into consideration." From under the conference table, he produced another large drawing of the back of the house. On the clear overlay he pointed out an huge multi-level deck, refurbished tennis courts along with a redesigned swimming pool and spa that looked just like a natural lake with plants and trees.

"These are just initial ideas, but I think if you retain the same number of guest rooms in the house, you can make this work without using too much more water or electricity to run it. Adding a small restaurant would be the major expense. He flipped down another overlay that showed a separate restaurant building. "What do you think?"

I thought he hated the idea of developing Dove Acres, but this was amazing. I felt a tear run down my cheek. I tried to wipe off with my finger before he saw it.

"I don't know what to say." I had no idea you were doing all this for me." I ran my hand across the drawing as his father came back in the room. "Why did you do all this? After what Jimmi and Jonnie said, I thought you gave up architecture."

Luke looked around the office before conceding, "Well, it's really not a big deal... I've changed my mind about a lot of things and besides, I have a lot of free time." The older Mr. Garrett nodded in agreement.

"At least let me pay you for the time you put in to this Luke."

He got that same twinkle in his eye that he had when he bet me about the flying fish, "You can repay me by following through with dinner on my boat."

I sighed, "You aren't going to let that bet go are you?"
He shook his head.

"All right..." I held out my hand to shake his, "in a couple of weeks." But instead of shaking my hand, he pulled me close, kissed me on the cheek and whispered, "Deal."

"Ahem," Luke's father let us know he was in the room.

I looked at the clock and remembered I had to get back to my presentation. We went back up to Dove Acres so Luke could get his cart. All the time I blabbered about the changes that the B&B would bring. He was very quiet and I just knew it took all he had to not say anything. I saw him off and walked into the house, excited to tell Veronica all about it until I saw my presentation papers were missing from the table. Tom's going to kill me! "Veronica?" I yelled and raced up the stairs.

Veronica appeared at the kid's room. "Where are the papers I had on the table?"

"Nicholas got into them."

"Oh shit."

"So... I moved them out of his reach." She handed them to me.

"I'm sorry I panicked, Veronica."

"While I was nursing April I happened to glance through them. I'm sorry to be nosy, but I added a few words here and there for you. Those college words were just impossible."

I scanned her changes, "Wow, this is much easier to read. By the way, do you know anything about good and bad cops?"

She shook her head then turned her attention to April. It was really bugging me, good and bad cops. I searched the internet but it didn't help. Veronica yelled from the top of the stairs. "Do you mean good cop/bad cop?"

"Yea, that's what Tom said."

"Oh, for goodness sakes, Maddie, that's a tactic two people use to throw off the other person or party in negotiations or presentations. One person is all kissy, huggy and the other comes across as the hardnosed Gestapo type. If you stay focused on what you have to say and ignore their game, you'll do fine." She held my hand, "My first husband, Jared was in real estate. Commercial property. Big stuff. Every time he went to arbitration or court, people would pull that."

I re-read the twenty-two items, rewording it into a story with a plot, introduction and I added a conclusion. This was how I organize my short stories and I think it will work. I could feel a heavy load leave my shoulders.

After I put my papers back in a safe place Veronica told me she had to go into Avalon and pick up some medicine for April's cough.

"I'll go with you. It's easier for two grownups to handle two bouncing toddlers and a sick baby, plus I can stop by the post office."

"Who'd like to go for a ride?" Veronica asked her little ones. They jumped up and down with excitement until Nicholas stopped and asked, "We eber gonna come back, Mommy?"

"Of course we're coming back. We're just going to the pharmacy with Auntie Maddie."

I tapped Veronica on the shoulder and whispered, "Auntie Maddie?"

"I didn't know what else to tell them. They're so little and it helps them feel more secure. Is that okay with you?"

"It's fine, Veronica." Being an only child I never thought I'd ever get called Aunt Maddie. "It's got a nice ring to it." I smiled, "don't you think?"

We stopped at the drug store, unloaded the children and went inside, while I went into the Post Office. That homeless guy was leaning against the wall inside the promenade. I got my mail and went back to the Pharmacy as Veronica was coming out the door, "The Pharmacist told us to come back in thirty minutes and it would be ready."

She herded her two little ones ahead of me and headed for the waterfront. "C'mon guys," she whispered to them, "Let's get some bottles and cans." She looked back at me, seemingly embarrassed by her statement.

"It looks bad, huh? Having little ones pick up cans and bottles."

"Hey, Veronica, it's good for the environment and it teaches them a work ethic. Who am I to judge?"

"Besides, they love to do that. The best pickings are down along the beach."

I swayed back and forth with April and watched as Veronica found a discarded grocery bag and started to pull out cans and plastic water bottles from the trash cans along the street for Nicholas and Sarah to crush with their feet. After it was full, Veronica tied the bag closed and squatted down next to Nicholas.

"Sweetie, I'm going to wait right here where I can see you. I want you to take this bag over to the car, toss it in the back window and come right back." With a little pat on the bottom she sent him running back to the Wagoneer. We watched as Nicholas tried twice to throw it high enough to get in the window, finally making it on the third try. He looked so proud when he turned around to come back, but something frightened him so bad that he screamed, "Mommy!" and started running towards us as fast as his little legs would carry him.

"Veronica, what is it?"

Suddenly we heard someone yell, "Hey Nicky, I thought that was you. Come back here you little snot." Veronica took a quick look over her shoulder and ran toward me in a panic. That dirty homeless guy in the camo jacket, strutted across the parking lot toward us. He pulled the lit cigarette stub out of his mouth, flicked it in the dirt. "Hey Ronnie," he yelled and broke into a run toward us, "The hell'er you doin' here?"

Veronica froze for a fraction of a second, "Hurry, hurry hurry." She looked back, grabbed Nicholas by the arm and ran to Sara scooping her up in her arms.

"Who is that?"

"It's my nutjob second husband and he found us. Oh my God! What am I going to do?"

"That creep?" I looked back at this person running toward us. "Come on, Veronica, get inside the Market, Now!" We rushed to the store up the three steps and into the Market. Veronica hustled the kids past Pinkie.

"Call the Sheriff Pinkie. A man is chasing us. And tell them to hurry!" I stuck a pacifier in April's mouth and held her close as we hid behind the meat counter. Pinkie dialed 911 and set down the receiver.

The man ran up the steps and threw open the doors, yelling, "Bitch, get back here. You're my wife. Where'd you go? Get out here now." From my hiding place I could see him over the steaks through the glass of the refrigerated case, he looked like he hadn't shaved in a couple of weeks and both his arms were peppered with tattoos.

Out of breath, Veronica whispered, "That's him alright."

I peeked around the corner of the aisle and watched. He looked left then right. When he did, the chain holding his wallet to his dirty old jeans jingled. He was searching for us with his beady little eyes. Cupping his hand by his ear, I could tell he was trying to hear the children's voices above the store music and refrigeration equipment. Pinkie stepped in front of him and in her firmest store manager voice she said, "Excuse me sir, can I help you with something?"

He stopped, swiveling his head around, he replied, "Nah, I'm cool."

"Well," Pinkie positioned herself squarely between him and the aisles. "I got air conditioning, so you want to turn around and shut those doors, please?" That broke his concentration. His shoulders drooped and he walked back to the front of the store. Pinkie, tried to distract him. "Is there something I can help you find?" He flipped her off and walked past her. The man methodically scanned the store and slowly paced across the front of the aisles, stopping to look down each one. We put our hands over the children's mouths and shushed them. As I peeked between the shelves, I could see Raylene in the candy and cookie aisle wearing a tight pair of red low-rise skinny jeans. She was bent over cutting open a case of cookies. He smiled a toothy grin and sauntered up the aisle toward her.

I handed April back to Veronica, "Take all the children. Go out through the loading dock in back and get back to the car," I whispered, "Drive around to the other side of the Arcade. I'll do something to stall him and meet you there." She nodded and quietly rushed away with her little ones. I stayed behind to keep an eye on the guy. Just as I predicted, he had been bushwhacked by his hormones.

"Hey, gorgeous." he said to Raylene, leaning on a shelf. Raylene looked under her arm. "What can I do for you?" She swiped her razor cutter along the top of the box. "You have got to be the prettiest thing I've seen all week." He leaned toward her, she leaned back. "Mmmmm, and you smell pretty too. You work here, I guess."

"Uh... duh." Raylene answered, still clutching the box cutter in her hand. "You think I do this for fun? What's your name, sailor?"

"Hey, how'd you know I have a boat?"

As I strained to hear their exchange, I couldn't believe how stupid this person really was. Raylene had no idea she was helping us by distracting this creep.

"Name's Little Lloyd, on account of my late daddy, Big Lloyd. He's buried back in Purgatory Springs, Missouri. But after you get to know me, you'll find out why the name's all wrong...."

Did he say Missouri? Could this idiot be my dopey third cousin Lloyd? I couldn't believe this was happening. He reached into his hip pocket and pull out a pack of Marlboros. Tapping out a cigarette, he hung it on his lip and went for his lighter.

"Sorry Killer," Raylene scolded, "You can't light up in here - it's against the law." She pointed to a large sign on the wall.

"Shit." he mumbled, "I hate California." He stuck the cigarette behind his ear and stuffed the pack back in his pocket. "So, whutchername sweet thang?"

"Raylene." She said, batting her baby blues.

He put one arm up on a shelf and leaned toward her. "You, like, married or got a boyfriend? Sumpin' like that?" She shook her head and flipped back her hair.

I looked at my watch. Veronica should be at the car by now. I then turned my attention back to Lloyd and Raylene's stimulating conversation.

"Hey, y'know I actually do got a boat here." Lloyd bragged.

"So? Everyone's here has a boat." Raylene shot back.

"Anyways, I can get us some beer and we can have a grand old time. Sit out on the water, fire up my little barbecue, cook up some burgers and knock back a few."

She sighed, looked up at the clock, then bent down and opened up the case of cookies.

From my hiding spot I could see him leer at her behind and lick his lips. She clicked the box cutter shut, stood and said, "Sure, free beer? What the hell, but good beer, none of that watery cheap crap."

"I'll get the beer and you meet me down by the Casino fuel dock." He grabbed a twenty-four can case of Masterbrau, looked at it for a moment and put it back. Instead he took a case of Heineken and went back up front to pay for it.

I quietly slipped out the same way as Veronica and went across to the arcade. Hiding in the shadow of the doorway, I watched him walk to where the Wagoneer had been parked, but it was gone. He stomped, and kicked the dirt. Obviously pissed that he let Veronica and the kids get away. I heard sirens I ran through the arcade, past the hardware store, Post Office and out the other side. I found Veronica in the Wagoneer with the engine running. She reached over and opened the door for me. I jumped in, buckled myself up while she headed for the Sheriff's Station. She whispered to me, "I sure hope they can't see their mommy's tears in the mirror, because when I saw his ugly face, I felt like I was going to throw up. But I was more frightened for the children. I mean, he traumatized little Nicholas when we were together."

Then we heard, "Hey bitch!"

Veronica and I looked around to see where it came from. In the outside rearview mirror I saw Lloyd jogging after the car.

"Come back here!" He shouted, "You can't hide on this rock. I'll find you." But he couldn't catch us as we drove away. Instead, he hurled a full can of beer at the car so hard it broke a tail light. The children screamed.

Veronica went a couple of blocks, turned left and pulled up right in front of the Sheriff's door. It was then we saw a sign taped to the glass, *Out on a call, be back shortly.* She took a deep breath, looked at me and turned to her crying children, "It's okay. We'll call the Sheriff when we get home."

"What am I going to do now Maddie?" Veronica whispered, "He knows we're here and he's seen my car."

"We'll be safe at the house." I assured her.

I opened the garage door and had her park in the one empty spot. We carried the now sleeping little ones into the house and laid them in their beds.

Veronica walked into the den while I was on the phone. I held up one finger to her. "Just a moment Deputy..." I put my hand over the mouthpiece, "What's the matter Veronica? You look like you're going to be sick."

The color drained from her face while she curled into a ball on the big chair and sobbed.

"I'm still here Sheriff... please hang on." I turned back to Veronica and said, "It's about my dopey third cousin, Lloyd Brewster. It seems he's here on Catalina."

In a panic, she looked up at me. "Lloyd Brewster is your cousin? Oh God, I gotta get out of here." She jumped to her feet. "The children! I have to get my children!"

I grabbed her arm and held it. "Stay put...." then turned back to the phone, "Don't hang up. I really need to talk to you, Deputy."

"What does this Lloyd look like, Ms Van der Wald? All we have are a couple of faxes of him when he was in high school"

"We saw him in town. He kinda looks like a homeless guy. He was smoking, thinning hair, missing a couple of teeth, wearing a camo jacket, dirty jeans, oh... and a chain on his wallet. He's maybe thirty. Let me look through my aunt's photo albums, maybe she has a more recent picture of him, and I'll call you."

I hung up the phone and hugged Veronica who was now sobbing and shaking.

"He's here and knows where I am. What am I going to do? What about my children? He's going to hurt my babies!"

"Nobody is going to hurt anyone. He might be the one digging up my property, probably looking for some non-existent treasure like in the stories Jojo told me... making noises outside at night trying to scare me off the island so he can inherit everything."

"But Maddie, if he comes back here, he'll find me and my children."

"Veronica, if he tries to come back here, we'll know. I had floodlights and an alarm system installed. If he gets anywhere near this place. Lights and sirens will go off... and as an added treat, he'll get his picture taken by security cameras and be met by the Sheriff. That will put him in jail. And since I've had it installed... we've had no more visits from the hole digger."

"That doesn't make me feel any better, I won't feel safe until he's locked up."

Waiting for the Sheriff to come, Veronica was watching the kids play on the floor. I remembered Dimple was expecting us for brunch tomorrow and changed the subject.

"Veronica, we need to get on with life. The Sheriff will catch him." She was silent.

"I've been invited to brunch at Dimple's place. You and the kids are invited."

"I can't go anywhere after what happened this morning."

"Please, do something fun. It will help the children get their mind off what happened. Besides, Lloyd can't find you if you aren't here."

Her head swayed a little looking at the kids. Then she smiled, "Is Dimple the funny lady with the big, black bun of hair on the top of her head and all the lipstick?"

She smiled but added, "We'd be imposing. Besides that, I've got nothing to wear for a Sunday brunch."

"I'm sure she'd love the extra company. I insist."

After a sleepless night with Veronica, I found a broomstick skirt and nice sweater for her to wear while she took a shower.

Afterward she said, "Since Jared died, I haven't had the desire or the opportunity to get dressed up or got makeup."

She stared into the mirror with a faraway look.

"Are you okay?" I asked.

"Oh sorry, I was just remembering how things were when Jared was with me."

We dressed the little ones in clean clothes. She fussed with little Sarah's hair until she looked like a princess and washed Nicholas's little face while giving him instructions for behavior. Little Sarah toddled into the room, grabbed Veronica around the leg and peeked from behind her skirt at the image her and her mother. "We pwetty."

It's easy to tell Veronica just needed another chance in life. People who've seen her living in that old Wagoneer with her kids don't know what a class act she really is.

"Everybody ready?" Veronica appeared at the top of the stairs holding Sarah's hand and carrying the baby. Nicholas bounded down the stairs ahead of them. "You look like a million dollars, Veronica. You all look great." I took the diaper bag and led the way to the garage, where we piled in the cart for the short drive to Dimple's house.

I introduced Veronica, Nicholas, Sarah and baby April to Dimple. She led the way and announced, "Everyone, I'd like you to meet some of our special guests, this is Nicholas," She patted him on the head. He vigorously announced, "I'm thix."

Dimple continued, "And young Miss Sarah, there behind her mother's skirt is going to be four. And this is her mother Veronica Christensen with her latest creation, April who is, four months old and of course, this is Maddie. I think you've already met her." I was shaking hands with Bryce and Stuart when a voice from behind me said "Maddie?"

It was Luke with a bid smile. "Fancy meeting you here." I stared at him for a minute.

Luke put his hand on my back and introduced me to Bryce and Stuart "These two are the nicest venture capitalists in the world." Jonnie and Jimmie bounced up to them, "Yep we can concur."

Dimple went around the table filling our glasses with lemonade,

"Veronica... " she said, "tell us a little about yourself."

Veronica replied, "Well, there's not much to tell. I grew up in Orange County. I'm widowed and I have three of the best children in the world."

I jumped in, "They're all wonderful children and they're staying with me at Dove Acres for a while."

Dimple went to the kitchen and returned with two small cups of lemonade for Nicholas and Sarah. She set them on the small table next to their own place cards while the children quietly colored away on the butcher paper. Dimple squatted next to them and softly asked, "Are we ready to eat?" Veronica seeing this, said "ahem, children..." and placed the palms of their hands together while she said a blessing on their food. Afterward they both looked up at their mother and smiled big toothy smiles.

"You have little angels." Dimple remarked as she passed freshly baked dinner rolls clockwise around the now silent table.

Rather than stare at my plate I broke the silence, "Tell me Jimmi, how did you and Bryce meet?"

"I'm a dental assistant. One day, Bryce came in to see Dr. Au for a root canal. The Doctor put him under and things were going along fine until he removed Bryce's crown. The porcelain cap popped out of the forceps and fell onto Bryce's lap. I tried to pick it but it slipped between his legs. When I reached down there to retrieve it, his eyes popped open. He jerked, I screamed and the crown slid further under him. My arm was caught between his thighs and he was squirming in the chair. I guess he thought I was trying to do something else. He grabbed my hand... anyway I think it was the anesthetic. It does weird things to people."

Bryce looked up at Stuart and Luke, winked and said, "...yeah, well we'll stick with that."

Veronica had not laughed for a long time, but she did. I turned to Jonnie, "How about you? How did you get hooked up with Stuart?"

She bit down on a carrot stick. "We really aren't hooked up. It just turned out that way. Wherever Bryce goes, there's Stuart with Jimmi and wherever she goes, you'll find me... except for shopping." Jonnie emphasized, "I don't do shopping."

Dimple scurried around the table collecting everyone's salad dishes. Pausing behind Jonnie, she said. "Actually, Jonnie is a master seamstress. Everything she's wearing, except her shoes, she made herself... even her jewelry."

Jonnie took a tiny sip of wine and replied, "Its a gift."

I noticed Jimmi's very expensive looking outfit and asked her, "Does Jonnie sew for you too?"

Jimmi's eyebrows went up about two inches at my comment and replied, "This is Chanel."

I felt everyone's eyes on me... Jonnie, Dimple, Jimmi, Veronica... even the guys. Totally embarrassed by my innocent question, I quietly stuffed a spoonful of potatoes in my mouth. I mean - like - I should know Chanel when I see it? Fortunately, Jimmi saved me from myself.

"While my dear sister Jonnie is multi-talented, and very good at what she does, I don't think she is up to the level of Chanel."

Jonnie rebutted, "What my sister isn't telling you, is where she bought her outfit... Jimmi is *The Queen* of consignment stores. I can't remember when she last set foot in a retail store."

"Pardon me, but I only shop at consignment shops in Beverly Hills, Santa Barbara, Laguna Beach, Malibu and Palm Springs. A lot of my things have celebrity pedigrees."

"Oh yeah, I forgot..." Jonnie chided, "It's famous trash." Jimmi threw a dinner roll in her direction. Dimple tapped the edge of her glass with the handle of her fork, "Okay, you two, manners, there are young ones watching."

"So how do you two guys know Luke?"

Bryce sat back in his chair and asked, "This slacker?"

Bryce went on, "Luke and I went to high school together. Those were some good times... I remember he really wanted to get into the Chicago Architectural Institute and worked really hard....but, I haven't seen much of him since he moved here to run the businesses with his father."

Stuart leaned toward me and asked, "Do you have any plans for Dove Acres?"

I snapped back, "Why is everyone so interested in what I'm doing with my property?"

He drew back in his chair as if I'd taken a swing at him.

I saw Luke smile.

Dimple cautioned Stuart, "I think you hit a nerve. Maybe you better not go there with Maddie just yet."

"Sorry Maddie, I'm very excited for you." Stuart continued, "I'm a venture capitalist, so if you ever decide to develop all or part of it for income producing purposes, here's my card."

Now I was embarrassed by my outburst and realized the golden opportunity just handed me. "Oh, Stuart, my apologies. You may be hearing from me when the time is right."

Bryce, Stuart, and the twins all looked at me with curiosity.

" I can't do anything with my aunt's estate for six months. Except maintain and upgrade it as needed. Thank you Stuart."

Luke sat quietly during brunch and just smiled or nodded. But he came alive at the mention of Dove Acres. "She's got some plans for the future though. Tell them about your B/B plans."

I couldn't take it anymore. "You know, I haven't really decided what I'm going to do. Everyone on this island seems to have plans of their own for me." I excused myself and went to the ladies room. I took a deep breath and decided it would be best if I left and not ruin the rest of Brunch. Dimple knocked on the bathroom door.

"I'm okay, but I have to go home and make – uh, phone call to the attorney."

"Luke wants to walk you home. Stuart is driving Veronica and the kids home.

"I can find my own way, thank you."

"He insists on it and with the prowler at large I think it would be safer for him to walk you home."

"Since you feel that way, please tell him I'll be right down."

"No, you tell him yourself. You've got to open the door to go through it."

I couldn't help but roll my eyes the way I did with my mother when she was ordering me around.

"Right now, he thinks you are a bit unbalanced. I suggest you get yourself collected and speak nicely to him."

"But Dimple..."

"Maddie, I told your Aunt Helen I watch over you if need be, and now that I have listened to you and Luke, I know there is something going on between you two young people. So, swallow your pride and talk to each other. I told him the same thing. Now I have to get back to my other guests... just do what I said and things will work out."

Chapter Ten

This was the big day and I was nervous about the meeting with Cellcom. The weather was beautiful, so I took a walk to help me collect my thoughts and go over the presentation in my mind. As usual I found myself near the cliff but to my surprise, I could see an inflatable boat with a big outboard motor pushed up on the little beach near entrance to the cave. This was probably the way whoever has been digging holes has been coming and going unnoticed. I looked back down at the tiny beach only to see a figure running from the path into the cave and out again. The person pushed the boat back into the surf, jumped in and sped off around the point to the west. I ran to where the path goes down to the beach.

There, behind a scruffy bush sat an orange wheelbarrow half full of dirt, two shovels with Dove Acres burned into the handles and a pair of work gloves. I continued along the cliff. In the distance I could see a small bay and moored in the center was a sailboat. I think it was the same boat I saw before. Tied up to it was the inflatable. I am definitely having a fence put up tomorrow. On the way back to the house I stopped at the stables where I found Javier brushing out Ricky.

"Javier, I saw a man running down the cliff trail. He climbed into a small rubber boat and sped away."

"What are you going to do *Señorita?*"

"I'm going to call the Sheriff's Department and report that trespasser, then I'm going to install a couple extra floodlights down near the cliff path until the Sheriffs catch this person. By the way, I found some shovels and wheelbarrow there. I think they're ours. Have you been missing any?"

"*Si Señorita*, I look for them yesterday and think, maybe I leave them by my garden, but they not there. I will get them."

"No, don't touch them, the sheriff will probably want to check for fingerprints."

I hurried back to the house and called the Sheriff. That is, after I checked all the doors and windows again.

When the doorbell rang I looked down from my window and saw the Sheriff's 4x4. Deputy Lopez and Malloy were standing at my door.

"The Sheriff is out of town until tomorrow and thought we should check this out right away."

While we drove out to where I saw the stranger run down the cliff path, I pointed out all the holes that had been dug along the way from the backseat of the 4x4, and showed them the shovels and wheelbarrow.

"I told Javier not to touch anything. I thought you might want to take fingerprints. Now let me show you where I saw the sailboat." I pointed out the little bay as we drove to the boundary with Dimple's property. The sailboat was still anchored there.

"That's the boat, but the inflatable boat is gone." I watched as the Deputies took more notes. "What are you going to do?"

"We'll investigate. Right now there's no crime. Nobody's actually seen the person dig the holes, Javier saw someone run away, and you saw someone get into a boat down on a public beach. None of your belongings have been removed from your property... the gloves, shovels and wheelbarrow are not stolen. They're still on your land, so there's no crime... yet."

Dumbfounded, I looked at them, "You're kidding, right? I live out here alone and you're not going to do anything?"

"Until a crime has been committed, we can't do anything." Deputy Lopez shrugged, "People have a right to do what they want, no matter how weird - as long as they aren't breaking any laws, Sorry."

We got back in the truck where Deputy Lopez apologized again. We stopped at a spot near the path where Deputy Malloy got out and took a couple of digital pictures of the gloves and tools left there.

"We'll have the Harbor Patrol check out that boat and see if we can find the inflatable. If we can find the owner... we'll have a chat and we'll get back to you. If anything changes, call us right away."

Deputy Malloy handed me his card. This didn't solve anything, but at least the Sheriffs are aware of the problem.

I walked into the house just as the phone rang. "Maddie, I saw the Sheriff's truck. Did you have another visit from your prowler?"

"Nothing like that Dimple. They only came up to take a report and get a description of the scene and the boat..."

"Wonderful. It's good to see them taking care of you. They're nice boys... the deputies."

"I have a meeting with some important people in a couple of hours and I'm real nervous."

"Think positive." I could hear my father in her voice.

Looking up at the clouds, I took a deep breath. Veronica called down to me from the bedroom window and motioned me upstairs.

She laid out a suit for me to wear this afternoon. She'd changed the black buttons on the green suit to gold, "I took them off another outfit you aunt had." Quite frankly it looked very nice. "You need to look professional," and she pulled my hair back with a couple of combs. It made me look thirty years old.

"I don't like it."

"You need to look professional and if it means looking older, that's a plus. Especially if you think they're expecting a fight."

That didn't make me feel any better. Even after a quick lunch, my nerves continued to get worse. "Here drink this." Veronica pushed a mug toward me. "It'll calm you down."

I stared in the mug and sniffed it. "What is it?"

"Chamomile tea, now drink."

She offered to drive me into town, but I knew she was scared Lloyd would find her.

Avalon was getting closer and my feet and hands were getting sweatier. I can't remember the last time I was this nervous where my stomach wanted to turn upside down.

Chapter Eleven

Outside the bank, I took a deep breath and counted to ten before climbing the stairs to the second floor. Tom was waiting in the conference room where he introduced me to the Cellcom representatives. Matthew had a pleasant voice and a nice smile but his face was crooked. I don't know how else to describe it. Slouched in a wheelchair was an old man named Mr. Hugaboom or something. I wiped my clammy, cold hands on the back of my skirt and shook their hands. They said nothing and I couldn't remember their names. As soon as we sat down, Matthew explained how impressed he was with the tour of Dove Acres. "It's not just raw land like other properties I've seen. You already have electricity out there at the stables. That makes this project a lot cheaper and easier." His eyes lit up each time he smiled. The man in the wheelchair kept writing figures on a piece of paper.

"We can of course, disguise the tower," Matthew suggested, "to blend with the landscape."

I tried to ask questions but every time I opened my mouth, Tom cut me off. Matthew had to correct him on several points. Soon they totally bypassed me and talking directly to Tom! Mr. Hugaboom or whatever his name was tried to light a piece of taffy with his cigarette lighter. He must be demented or have Alzheimer's disease.

"Dad, let me have that," Matthew took the lighter out of his hand.

"Excuse me." I interjected, "This land has been entrusted to me by my great aunt to ensure her dream and plans continue. Dove Acres is a lovely place and I want to share it with people. This tower could help both of us, but its not going to happen without my approval. Dove Acres will go on with or without CellCom. I make the final decision."

I wrote a dollar amount for a monthly rental fee on a piece of paper with my name in large letters. "Call me if you're interested." I wanted to run screaming out of the room. But I needed to make the deal work, somehow. I stood and shook hands with each one of them, said goodbye and left the conference room in the most confident way I could. Tom ran outside after me and grabbed my arm. "What did you do? You just..."

"Don't tell me I blew the meeting. I crammed and prepared for this stupid presentation. You were supposed to be there to help and give advice, but you dominated the meeting like this was your property. Honestly, I don't think those men took me seriously and I think they were weird and flaky."

He let go of my arm, "I wanted to do right by you and Helen, I promised her I'd look after you and Dove Acres. So I'm doing that."

"By disrespecting me like that?"

He looked away. "I just want the best for you and Dove Acres. Helen meant a lot to my father and me and I wanted to do right by her."

"You mean her money meant a lot to your firm." I frowned, "Well, aren't you going to apologize?"

"No, I still think this is the best solution."

"You're so arrogant that you can't even apologize when you've screwed up? Are you lawyers missing a gene or something?"

I turned to walk away but he held my arm again. "I didn't mean to disrespect you in front of those people."

"Fine, they have my numbers. It's up to them - let's see how bad Cellcom wants this spot. Call me when you hear anything from them."

My head was pounding, but at least Nicholas and Sarah were happy to see me when I got home.

"I had some grown-up stuff to do," I told them, "but I really missed you guys." Though my head throbbed I squatted down and gathered them into my arms for a big hug.

Veronica leaned in from the kitchen, "Your friend Jojo called. She said she has something important to tell you and that she'd be stopping by later."

When I stood up my head felt like it wanted to pop. I closed my eyes for a moment.

Veronica asked, "Are you okay?"

I shook my head. "Not really. This whole running an estate thing is a pain and now I understand why everyone hates lawyers."

She replied, "If there is an upside, it would be that a cell tower would just sit there. Kind of like a money machine. Nobody running around, it wouldn't make noise or pollute the land like an oil well, and all you have to do is cash the rental checks from Cellcom for who knows how long."

"I guess maybe I should just do what Tom says and get it over."

While I was upstairs washing my face, I heard a cart pull up on the gravel driveway. Out the window I saw Jojo carrying a couple big books and a small package.

"Whatcha got?" I gave her a hug, which she didn't return. She shook her head and put the books down on the table.

"I found something important about our land." and opened the small paper wrapped package. Inside were the shell arrowheads we found in the cave. "I showed these to the head of Native American History at the University in San Bernardino. She said these were most likely from a burial site on the island. You know what that means?"

"So, there IS Indian treasure buried around here."

"No, Maddie. It means you can't erect a cell phone tower here. You'd be desecrating sacred native lands and that's a Federal crime."

This is NOT turning out to be a very good day.

"Well, who has been digging up this sacred native land? Have your Native American friends been up here planting artifacts so I can't build anything?"

"What? How could you say such a thing?"

"Javier and I found shovels and work gloves up here near the cliff above the cave where you and I supposedly discovered those shell arrowheads. And I saw a rubber boat on the beach by the cave. I called the Sheriffs and they're investigating all this."

Jojo gathered up her books and shells, "I thought I could talk to you like a sister but you are acting just like them."

"Them? What them? Where are you going?"

"Your parents. You sound just like them. I knew I was never a part of your family. This proves it." Jojo headed for the front door. "This isn't finished. You'll be hearing from me soon - Ms. Van der Wald."

I didn't really want to talk to Tom right now but this was important, so I called his cell. It just rang and rang. "Come on Tom, pickup - please." I left a voice mail and hoped he would call back soon.

"Why is this happening, Veronica?"

"Life isn't so bad Maddie. There are some things we can't control. How we handle those things is what makes the difference. Believe me, I know."

I took a deep breath. "You're right. I can only deal with the things I can change. So, I'm going to the Sheriff's office and see if they have any information on Lloyd. Veronica was too afraid to come so I went alone. Deputy Lopez was at his desk on the phone with the Sheriff. I waited and wondered if Lloyd was still on the island.

I explained to the deputy what happened in town, he listened politely and took notes.

"We ran a background check on Lloyd Brewster. We don't have any arrest record on him in California."

I couldn't believe this guy was a model citizen.

"But back in Missouri," The deputy read, "he has a long list of offenses, including a few for vehicle theft and fraud, and a couple for assault. The Harbor Patrol checked out any boats resembling the one you saw by the cave and found one that's been missing from the Terminal Island marina for over a month, but no one reported it stolen until the day before yesterday."

This was scary but I didn't want Veronica to know they hadn't caught him yet.

"Deputy Malloy went out with the Harbor Patrol to question the skipper of *The Slippery Eel*, that was the name on the transom."

He reported no one on board, but they found credit card receipts and a bunch of mail on board, addressed to Lloyd Brewster, General Delivery, Avalon, California.

"That's definitely Little Lloyd. I just know he's trying to scare me off the island. If I don't stay here for the term of my aunt's will he gets the estate."

I pulled a copy out of my purse and read aloud, "If I don't fulfill my responsibility according to the will, I quote, '*the entire estate will default to the only child of my cousin Elizabeth (Bessie). Lloyd Brewster of Purgatory Springs, Missouri.*' end of quote. That's him, my dopey third cousin."

"We'll do what we can to catch him." But he stressed, "Until we catch him in the act of doing something wrong we can't arrest him. We can keep an eye on him, which really doesn't amount to much, but at least I know who to look for."

That was not reassuring at all.

"Miss Maddie, I called the County Sheriff in Purgatory Springs and asked if they wanted to extradite him back there to face these charges."

"Great. You can send him back there and they'll put him in prison, right?"

"Not really. They'd have to pay to transport him and frankly, they don't want him back, so we'll have to deal with him."

I flopped down in the chair across from him and sighed, "Are you kidding?" I shook my head, "and now I'm even sure he's the one digging up my property."

"It's a long story. I'll tell you later."

"I think you better tell me now. What's going on?"

"My adopted sister Jojo Ruiz, well she wasn't legally adopted. My parents took her in. Anyway, we found some shell arrowheads down in the cave, which she took and had checked out by the University. Now she claims that my property is a sacred Tongva burial site, but I think she may have put her Native American friends up to digging up the ground and planting this stuff just because she wasn't mentioned in my Aunt's will."

Deputy Lopez took notes, "Well this does complicate things, but Maddie, just like the situation with Lloyd Brewster, we need evidence to proceed any further. Hearsay just doesn't cut it."

"I don't know what to do Deputy. I was happy minding my own business back in L.A. until my Aunt passed, and now I have these huge problems and no one to help me except you."

"Listen, Miss Van der Wald - Maddie. We'll do what we can. You be sure to call right away if anything strange happens and we'll be right there."

For some reason, that didn't make me feel any better.

Chapter Twelve

 Veronica had strict instructions that I was not to be disturbed because I planned to work on my novel – well, except for lunch and supper of course. With her and the little ones here, I was able to keep from going crazy while I crossed each day off the calendar toward the time when Dove Acres was officially mine. Maybe I was supposed to learn something from all this.

 When I wasn't working on my novel, or surfing the web looking for online college classes, I'd select a book to read from one of my aunt's bookcases. Thankfully, she loved reading, and my aunt's collection was as varied as her experiences. I could spend days reading books but I've got to figure out how the heroine in my book is going to deal with this hot French lover who is trying to unlace the back of her dress. After all my research, the big thing I'd learned was that as late as the early nineteenth century, women were not treated a whole lot different than servants or livestock. Sure, some of their spouses loved them, but a lot of marriages were really business or political arrangements and the women were just pawns with no power or voice. Since this is fiction and since I'm the author, I can make her as spunky as I want and she can tell this Frenchman exactly how she feels. My fingers flew across the keyboard as I typed *"You must not speak to me in that manner! You only own this land because you married into it. My father shall hear of your poor treatment of his favorite daughter. Make no mistake about that! You may find yourself on a ship bound for France with nothing to show for your time here except for a bruised ego."* Now that's my kind of heroine. One who stands up for herself. Four hours and two chapters later, Veronica knocked softly on the door with a tray of lunch for me.

 "Where are Nicholas and Sarah?"

"I told them you were busy writing a story and that you could not be bothered or else your story would not be very good. They went outside on the verandah and started drawing pictures to help you."

That was so sweet. Maybe someday I might decide to have some of my own. This must be why mothers are all so mushy and corny after they give birth.

She set the tray on the edge of the desk and reminded me to stand up and walk around once in a while after I'd eaten. I thanked her and opened the window to let in a fresh breeze then went back to work until the sun began to set. I stopped for the evening and put the laptop away in a desk drawer.

The aroma of Veronica's cooking lured me to the kitchen where I peeked under the pot lids to see what smelled so good when she walked into the kitchen.

"That's for tomorrow. It's a seafood stew, but have some if you're hungry. I just put the children down for the night." Veronica said, "How goes the writing? Did you get those characters into a romantic situation yet?"

"I may need to do some more hands-on research on the subject."

"And how are you going to that? Or should I say with whom?"

"Oh, I don't know yet. When this waiting period is up, maybe I can head back to the mainland where there are more potential research partners."

Suddenly the sirens of my new alarm system went off for the first time. With my heart pounding in my head, we hurried upstairs to the bedroom that faced the ocean and opened the drapes. The security lights lit up the property and we could see the Coast Guard boat. Their blue and red lights were flashing while bright white searchlights scanned our house and circled the area like some Hollywood movie premiere.

"Mommy! Mommy!" Sarah and Nicholas came screaming into the room.

Veronica scooped up Sarah and hugged Nicholas close to her.

"Where's April?"

I ran to the other room and brought her in.

We could hear a loudspeaker, but couldn't understand the words.

I called 911 but I got a message to leave my name and number. It said they would get right back to me.

The sound of glass breaking downstairs startled all of us. I opened the door and went into the hall.

"There's someone in the house." I whispered, "Everyone be quiet. I'll be right back."

I crept to the hall closet and looked around for something - anything to defend myself. There was nothing except an old floor lamp and a baseball bat. I took off the shade and held it like a lance. I tiptoed back to the room and handed the bat to Veronica. She stared at me like I was nuts.

I pointed my makeshift lance at the door, ready to lunge.

"What are you doing?" Veronica asked.

"Never mind what I'm doing. Just stay behind me."

Nicholas and Sarah covered their eyes and squealed. Veronica sat them on the floor facing the corner.

I peeked in the hall, "Stay in here and keep the door closed. I'm going to see what's going on."

"Please be careful." She whispered. The sound of a car outside and loud voices came from downstairs.

Veronica opened the door and looked at me in terror, "It's Lloyd! I hear his voice."

I ducked back inside and tried to calm her with a hug. April began crying and the other children were whimpering. Nicholas asked, "What wrong mommy?"

I peeked out the window. The Sheriff's deputies were going around the side, toward the kitchen, and coming from the cliffs were three or four people with bright flashlights running toward the house.

"Everybody stay down on the floor behind the bed." I whispered before crawling over to the door to hear what was going on.

Deputy Lopez shouted, "You, Brewster, get on the floor, face down with your arms out - you're going to jail!"

Lloyd screeched back, "Yeah? You and what army? C'mon pretty boy I can take you."

"Put the knife down Brewster." The deputy shouted, "You're just making more problems for yourself."

There was loud banging and thumping then a lot of voices, scuffling, shouting and the sounds of things breaking.

Suddenly everything was quiet. I slowly opened the door and crept on my stomach over to the stairs. Through the railing I saw Lloyd downstairs laying face down on the floor with his hands handcuffed behind his back. Deputy Malloy was standing over him reading him his rights. I looked up. Above me, Deputy Lopez extended his hand to help me up.

"What's happening down there?"

"I'll explain. Come downstairs, I need you to sign the incident report."

Veronica listened from the top of the stairs as I asked the deputy how they knew Lloyd came here. He told me the Coast Guard made a second sweep of the area just before sunset when they spotted a bright orange object on the beach below the property.

"They called us to come out and investigate since it was on County land."

"Did you ever get my 911 call?" I asked.

They shook their head.

"When we arrived at your gate we got a radio call from the Coast Guard that they spotted someone running up the path toward your house and sent some men ashore."

"How do you know he won't get away?" I asked.

"He's in shackles now, and he's going to stay that way." The Deputy assured us, "We'll take him down to jail in Avalon tonight. After this little stunt, I'll call the judge. He's on the island right now and maybe we can get this guy arraigned in the morning."

Veronica cautiously came down the stairs with her three little ones. April had calmed down while Nicholas and Sarah followed behind her one step at a time. Nicholas tugged at Deputy Lopez's leg. He looked down at him and rubbed the top of his head.

"How you doin' little buddy? Aren't you up kinda late?"

Nicholas shook his head. "I wathn't thcared."

The sergeant bent down and unbuttoned his shirt pocket. "You know what? I think I have something for you." He produced a gold metallic sticker that looked just like a sheriff's badge and stuck it on the front of Nicholas' pajamas. He beamed with pride and showed his mother. The deputy put another one on Sarah's nightshirt. "There you go young lady. You can help your brother."

Veronica hugged her children and thanked the deputy for their stickers.

"You know," Deputy Lopez remarked, "After what you told us before, if Brewster was after you Ms. Van der Wald, I hate to think what he had planned for Veronica and the children."

"Lloyd's really going to jail?" Veronica asked.

He nodded, "Yes Ma'am, and with all the previous crimes on his record, you can bet he won't be bothering you or Ms. Van der Wald for a long time." Dimple came running into the house with another deputy running after her.

"Maddie you okay? I heard and saw all the fuss. What happened?"

Shards of broken glass from the door littered the kitchen floor. The table was on its side. The chairs were thrown across the room and everything that was on the table was now on the floor.

"Oh my God!" Dimple gasped. "Let me help you clean this all up." She turned to the two deputies, "Would you boys help us put the door back up?"

"Sorry for the mess Ms. Van der Wald. Mr. Brewster will have to pay for all the broken items. It will be in the report."

"Aren't those deputies nice young men?" Dimple remarked, "I've known them since they were in high school."

An hour or so later, I left Dimple downstairs and went back up to the bedroom where Veronica was cuddling her little ones.

She sighed, "I'm so relieved."

But I could tell she was putting on a strong face for the children. We brought them down for a snack of warm milk and muffins. While Dimple split a muffin and put half on each of their plates, Veronica and I stood near the sink.

"You know," Veronica whispered so the children couldn't hear, "We'll probably have to leave the island soon."

I looked at her with disbelief and whispered back, "Whatever for? Lloyd's been arrested. "You have a place to stay here. Why would you leave?"

"Now that Lloyd knows where we are Maddie, there isn't any place to hide on this island, and he won't be in jail forever. He'll know where to find us anytime he wants to cause trouble."

This wasn't how this was supposed to work. She can't leave now. Where would she go? Where would they live? And most importantly, who would cook? I'll starve!

"I've got plans for Dove Acres Veronica... and you're in them. I want you to stay. You'll be safe here. You have friends here. We'll get a restraining order for both of us."

Dimple added, "Veronica dear, you can't keep uprooting these children. They need a stable home and Maddie is willing to provide one for them... and you."

I nodded, "fall will be coming and winter. Anyway, what're you going to do on the mainland? I'm your friend and this is the ideal place for you and the kids."

Dimple looked at us and put her finger to her lips, "Listen. Peace has come to Dove Acres."

I hadn't really noticed the quiet. It was more a lack of noise, but Dimple was right. I felt a giant weight lifted from my shoulders.

The next morning I got a call from the Sheriff's office and I knew Veronica wasn't going to like what I had to tell her.

"We need to go to the Jail to positively identify Lloyd and fill out a formal complaint. You don't have to come if you don't want to."

"Are you kidding, Maddie? Of course! I want to make sure he's behind bars."

Veronica pushed open the front door of the Sheriff's office like a woman on a mission. "Where is he?" she demanded, "I want to make sure it's him, so I can file an assault complaint."

Deputy Malloy calmed her down, "Mr. Brewster is locked safely away behind those doors in a holding cell." He showed her to a table where he handed her a pen and a stack of forms. "First, you need to fill out the complaint."

I sat next to her with my own set of forms. By the time we finished writing down all the details of our encounters with Lloyd, I had writer's cramp.

"Okay, let's go positively identify the perpetrator." Deputy Lopez unlocked the door and escorted us down the hall and through another locked steel door to the holding cells. Lloyd, still handcuffed, stuck his head up to the bars to see who was coming and yelled, "I want a lawyer, get me outta here, I didn't do nothin'."

"Sir," Deputy Lopez commanded, "Please step back, sit down and shut up." He held his hand up for us to wait where we were.

Barefooted, Lloyd slunk back onto the cot and stared at the deputy like he wanted to kill him. The deputy motioned for us to wait along the wall opposite the cell.

As soon as Veronica saw him sitting there, she shook her head and commented, "Yes sir, that is definitely Lloyd Brewster Junior of Purgatory Springs, Missouri and, if he would sign the divorce papers, my ex-husband."

Lloyd looked up at us and shouted, "Hey bitch, you're still my wife. What'er you trying to do, frame me? That's my wife out there deputy, Ronnie, tell'em I'm yer husband.

Disgusted, Veronica looked at Deputy Lopez, "He still has that mouth. I filed for divorce from him months ago," she looked back at Lloyd, "But he won't sign the papers and I am not bailing him out. That's for sure!"

I stepped up and took a look. He glanced up and saw me. "Oh, well, if it isn't her highness, the rich and mighty Miss Madeline Van der Wald... you spoiled little bitch, I should have killed you when I had the chance. You don't deserve any of that land, you already have everything, I don't have nothing. It ain't fair, it just ain't frickin' fair. There has to be sumthin' in that old house 'cause There wasn't anything buried out there. I dug that whole frickin' place up and for what? Nuthin! I want a lawyer."

Shaking his head, the deputy said, "Okay, that'll do." and escorted us down the hall closing the big steel door which muffled the sound of Lloyd's yelling. "His arrest record is full of unresolved charges that he'll have to answer for."

"Thank God," Veronica said, "The man is a menace." Deputy Lopez escorted us out to the office. In the next few days we are going to need some statements, and I'm sure when Brewster gets an attorney, they're going to want to talk to you."

"Can we go now?"

The deputy nodded.

Chapter Thirteen

I called Tom and told him about the trouble with Lloyd.

"Your third cousin Lloyd Brewster is there... on the island?"

"Yes, and since you are the executor, how does this affect the terms of the will? He stalked and chased my guest Veronica and scared her children, and broke into the house all while trying to scare me away."

Tom sighed, "Did you say this Lloyd Brewster has been arrested and is in jail there in Avalon?"

That was weird. He sounded...not so much surprised as disappointed by the news. "Uh, why on earth would he be stalking your friend Veronica and chasing after her kids?"

"It turns out that my Lloyd is her estranged husband. Small world, huh? I would never have guessed."

"Hmm, is that so?"

"Well Tom? Is there something you can do, like get a restraining order on him? Does this disqualify him from inheriting Dove Acres? The guy is a criminal and now he's in jail... what can you do?"

"Hmmm. I'll go through the will and research that. When I see you tomorrow, I'll let you know what I found out."

"Tomorrow? Are you coming out here?

"No, You're coming over here. The Cellcom people are ready to sign the contract if you are. I'll pick you up at the boat landing in Serena Beach at one p.m. tomorrow.

The next morning I put my laptop and knock-off Louis Vuitton overnight bag by the door. I left a message with Dimple to check on Veronica. The Sheriff's office had my cell phone number and Lloyd was locked up. I checked on Javier and the horses. When I looked at the clock, I was shocked to see it was almost eleven o'clock. I didn't have much time to get my ticket and board the eleven forty-five boat.

Tom picked me up in Serena Beach and drove me to a hotel, a nice one in Beverly Hills. I asked if he had a solution for the Lloyd problem. His response was, "I haven't had time to look over the will. My time has been taken up with this deal and some other cases I have."

"Well, when will you know? The Sheriff said they are going to arraign Lloyd today and I want all of the charges against him made public. You promised to go over the will."

"I'll do what I can Maddie."

"Tom. I want a restraining order on this flake ASAP. This is important!"

I didn't speak to him again until we arrived at the hotel, I left my bag with the Bell Captain, assuming we were going to have lunch and go over the contract before the meeting, instead he took me to a private suite with a meeting room.

I positioned myself on a Queen Anne chair near the window while Tom arranged papers on the meeting table. Someone knocked on the door. "Is that the people from Cellcom already?" I wished we had talked about it or let me read the contract first. Tom grinned as he opened the door.

"Room service, Sir - The champagne you ordered."

"Put in on the meeting table," Tom ordered, "and set out glasses." The bellman placed the two large bottles of champagne in silver ice buckets and set them by the head of the table.

"What's all this for?" I asked, "Isn't it a bit early to celebrate? I haven't even seen the final contract."

Tom busied himself positioning the glasses in front of each binder on the table and rewrapping the towels around the champagne bottles to keep them chilled.

"No problem, Maddie, I've already read them over. All that's left is for you - er, us to sign them."

"Hold on there Mr. Silverman. You've already seen it and didn't tell me what the deal is I'm making with these people? I may be young but I am not completely stupid. My father taught me never to sign anything I haven't read or with blanks that aren't filled in."

"But Maddie, it's all very cut and dried. Standard contract stuff - pretty dull."

"I don't care. I am not signing anything until I've read it. Now, do you have a copy of this contract with you?"

I could see sweat on his forehead and his face got red.

"Well..." he stammered and fumbled with his briefcase, "... actually I do."

He leafed through the papers in his briefcase while I stared at him. He glanced up at me periodically, "I know I have one here..."

"You better, because I am NOT doing anything until I've read it."

"You probably wouldn't understand much of what it says."

"You don't know that. Anyway, I'll ask them what it means. I am insulted. Now give me the contract." I held out my hand.

He pulled the packet out and slowly held it out to me.

"Let go so I can read it."

"Before you read it, I just want to say..."

There was another knock at the door.

I glared at him, "We'll talk about this later."

At the door was the man with the crooked smile, Matthew, he brought his briefcase and yet another bottle champagne.

I pulled Tom aside. "I'm sorry, but you're all going to have to keep yourselves busy this afternoon until I've have had time to go over this."

"Sure, Maddie."

The contract was twenty seven pages long and I had no idea what most of it said. "Remember Maddie, any contact can be negotiated. Anything you want changed we can discuss. Matthew began talking to Tom as he sat down on the sofa.

"Excuse me," I thumbed through the pages. "but I'm not sure I can get his digested right now. I'll need more time. Tell you what. I'll take the rest of the day to go over this. Maybe we can meet again first thing in the morning."

Matthew's smiled faded quickly. Tom was speechless. "Let me go through this with you." Matthew suggested, "and Tom can listen to be sure I'm on the mark, and answer any questions you may have."

Tom opened the champagne and poured three glasses.

"You may as well put that away until tomorrow." I said, opening the first page. "and Tom, you better get a room for yourself. Now if you gentlemen will excuse me, I have some reading to do."

They gathered their things and turned toward the door.

"Oh," I added, "Don't forget to take all that champagne with you, and please close the door."

"Maddie, I..." Tom began.

I held up my finger, "If I have any questions, I have all your cell numbers."

They closed the door and left me alone. I called down to the front desk and had my bags brought up, then I ordered lunch from room service, making sure to charge everything to Tom's account.

I read in the contract where Matthew added a few things such as building a new stable some distance from the tower at their expense. That was good. They'd pay all liability insurance coverage for the property around the tower in the event of a collapse, temporarily give up all mineral rights to the property for the period of the lease. "Basically," I mumbled to myself, "the company is renting my land for twenty years."

The next morning when I met with them, they were both very quiet.

"Y'know, I couldn't find where I could cancel the agreement. It is an option, right?"

"Sure," Matthew began, "it's in the contract," and showed me the section. It didn't exactly state the ending date of the lease. Tom explained it was there.

"We'll need to postpone signing the contract until it is more clearly written," I insisted.

Tom was irritated, Matthew seemed a bit disappointed. I felt like I was the one leasing the land. If truth be told, I felt more like I was buying a car.

"Cellcom has spent a lot of money and time already and they planned to begin the project in two weeks."

"Well, then add an amendment and overnight it to me, "If it looks good, I'll sign both documents."

"Maddie, just sign the contract, we can always amend it later," Tom insisted. "I promise. It will take time to put an amendment together."

"I'm sorry, but I told you my rule about signing things."

Matthew organized the papers on top of his briefcase. Tom was visibly agitated and asked for a private moment with me. Matthew excused himself and left the room.

"I know this is important step for you Maddie. But I assure you this is all above board and perfectly legal. I checked every portion of the contact myself, twice. Why would you want to cancel the lease before it's up?

"There are a million reasons, and I have to leave myself an out. What if I want the land back for development?"

He explained that the company was putting a great deal of money into the project. "Ending the lease would require a notice of two or three months and they would try everything to renegotiate it. If you're uncertain you better tell us - er, them now. A lot of time and effort on my part and theirs have already gone into putting this deal together."

"So? Besides, aren't you supposed to be looking after my welfare?"

"I am!" His voice got louder, but he caught himself and closed his eyes.

"Look Tom, I'm not signing this contact as is. You're MY lawyer, not theirs. Act like it!"

"Let me talk to Matthew, he's probably at the bar."

I never had to argue with a lawyer before and I was shaking after he left. I wished I could call Jojo but she is pissed at me. I just didn't know what to do. I took one of Matthew's copies off the top of his briefcase and shoved it into my overnight bag.

The next morning as I stepped off the boat, there was Veronica and the kids. Sarah, in her princess nightgown and Nicholas, in his superhero pajamas ran up and hugged me round the knees. "I mith you bery, bery much." We stopped by the post office after we left the dock. Included in my mail was a letter inviting me to a meeting Monday morning at the bank where I first met the Cellcom people. It was signed, Mr. T. Woodfin, President. I hope it's not bad news. I'd never met a bank president before, but Dimple trusted Mr. T Woodfin explicitly. She called him "Woody." Maybe he just wants to talk about really boring stuff about things like annuities or retirement or investment strategies or other things I don't really understand.

As I was getting unpacked I told Veronica about my adventures.

"It sounds like you did very well for yourself. I'm proud of you." Her compliment made my heart jump. I hadn't had anyone say they were proud of me since my parents died.

After sorting through the two days worth of mail I needed to stretch, so I took some carrots out of the refrigerator, and headed for the stable. I saw Lucy in the corner. She looked very weak and shaky with the cast on her damaged leg. She whinnied so I stepped in her stall and held a carrot out to her. She gobbled it up. Ricky, Fred and Ethel were munching hay as I came in. While I fed them, they nudged me in the back and rubbed their snout on my arm. They seemed to sense I was heartbroken. Being betrayed and losing a friend is hard for anyone. "Well," I told Ethel, stroking her mane, "You can always trust Lucy, Ricky, Fred and me."

I couldn't sleep and went to the kitchen for warm milk and cookies while I flipped through a copy of Island Life magazine. After a second cookie, I tiptoed upstairs. All three little children were peacefully sleeping away.

As I passed Veronica's room, her door was open and her room was empty. Her bed wasn't disturbed. I thought that very strange, since she usually goes to sleep when her kids do. She wasn't in the bathroom. Maybe she was on the patio. My search continued around the side of the house to the driveway where I discovered Veronica laying on her back on the roof of the Wagoneer, her arms spread out. It looked very weird. Silently, I crept up close and whispered, "Veronica." She let out a gasp, bolted upright and shouted, "Dammit, Maddie, you scared the Hell out of me. Don't ever do that again. Just call my name or something before you're right up on me. Okay?"

"I'm sorry, but why in the world are you on top of your car?"

"I was looking at the stars, and thanking God that you're here for us."

I put one foot on the front bumper and pulled myself onto the hood, then stepped carefully across the fender. Veronica grabbed my hand and helped onto the driver's side of the roof. We giggled as I climbed over the luggage rack and wiggled up next to her.

Together we gazed at the clear night sky. There was no moon but so many stars I felt I could reach out and scoop them up in my hand.

"This is great."

She nodded and put her hand in mine.

We laid there in silence for some time, gazing into the night sky until she looked over at me. I wish she hadn't.

"You're crying Maddie." I'm sure Veronica knew all about tears. She turned on her side, propped herself up on one elbow, "Are you okay?"

"I guess so... I was thinking about my problems."

"What happened?"

I told her how upset I was at what Tom did at the meeting back in L.A.

"Sometimes I think he's just in this for the money, which he probably is. I thought he was a friend of the family, not just some asshole lawyer. He just seems so stereotypical."

"I know..." She remarked, "I was married to an asshole. They should all be locked up. For what it's worth, I learned one important concept from those relationships." She whispered, "Whatever you do or want to do, you have to live with the decisions you make."

That's what Dimple said.

"Maddie... you're a resourceful young woman, I know you'll find a creative solution." She turned her attention back to the stars. We stayed up there for a long time, saying nothing, taking in the wonder of the universe.

It was almost midnight when we finally climbed off the car and went back in the house, but my mind was racing. I decided to do what my mother always told me to do when I couldn't sleep. I got pencil and paper, and made a list of everything on my mind. I tried again to stop worrying. Finally after wrestling with my pillow until two in the morning, I drifted off to sleep.

The clock said ten-thirty in the morning when I opened my eyes. Veronica was doing the dishes as I stumbled into the kitchen where she had a quiche cooling on the counter.

Outside someone was blowing their car horn. At first I wondered who could be parked in my driveway making all that racket until I heard, "Yoo Hoo! Yoo Hoo!" It was Dimple. I'd forgotten I gave her the code for the gate in case of an emergency, but I'd still recognize that "Yoo Hoo" if we were in Times Square on New Year's Eve.

I leaned out the kitchen window and heard her say, "I'm driving up to the airport to collect my nieces and their friends. They just flew in from Rancho Mirage and they're all coming up for dinner tonight. Would you join us?"

I nodded. She waved, then got back into her big Ford Galaxy and drove away.

Chapter Fourteen

That evening Veronica brought along some scones, strawberry preserves and something called Devonshire Cream.

At dinner I proudly told everyone how I stood up for myself. "It took all my courage to confront Tom and Matthew but I did it and made Tom agree to do what I wanted. He tried to take over the whole meeting, but I wouldn't let him"

In the middle of my story, Victor Minotti walked into the dining room. "What the hell is he doing here?" I hoped I hadn't said that out loud. With my best fake smile, I gritted my teeth and greeted him while trying to be as civil and composed as possible.

"Victor, what a surprise. Why are you here?"

Before answering, Victor turned to Jimmi and Jonnie "You didn't tell me you had such beautiful neighbors."

Jonnie commented, "I get the idea you two know each other. For goodness sakes Maddie, aren't there any young guys you don't already know?"

"We used to be a couple." Victor bragged.

"We went out twice." I held up two fingers and corrected him, "I don't call that being a couple... and that was over a year ago."

"Well," Dimple stepped between us, "Since you two have already met, let me finish the introductions... Veronica, this is Bryce Phillips... he's with Jimmi. And this is Stuart Mortensen... He belongs to Jonnie."

Stuart cleared his throat, "We date." Jonnie hit him in the shoulder.

I stood, "For the benefit of everyone here, I knew Victor Minotti in Santa Ana when I was a senior in high school. We met at a mall. I think he was working at that pizza place for little kids with the big Rat costume, he was the rat in the costume. We only went out twice." Again I held up two fingers, "But I'm curious Victor. How did you meet these nice people?"

Victor explained while his eyes zoomed in on Veronica, that he was caddying for Bryce and Stuart at the Rancho Mirage Country Club a couple of days ago.

Bryce interrupted, "Victor seemed like a good kid so we invited him to come along. I didn't know there was any history between you two."

Dimple deftly switched Veronica's and my place settings, so I wasn't sitting next to Victor. She had also set up a small card table covered with butcher paper and a supply of crayons for the children. April had fallen asleep with her bottle.

Dimple's phone rang. She returned and whispered in my ear, "Maddie dear, it's that attorney, Tom calling for you."

Surprised, I looked up at her. "He's calling me? Here at your home? I'm so sorry Dimple."

"Well it must be important. You can use the phone in the kitchen, through that door."

When I stood, Victor remarked, "Don't worry Maddie, I'll entertain them with stories about us until you get back."

I rolled my eyes, "Oh please don't."

I took a deep breath, "Why are you calling me here? Just what do you want?"

"Still pissed off I see," Tom said, "I was checking to see if you were okay and..."

I hung up on him and went back to the others.

"Maddie, we all got off track here. You were telling us about this contract, "Bryce commented, "do you happen to have a copy with you?"

I still had the copy in my purse. Bryce asked if he could see it. "Sure. I'd like you to look at it. I just don't trust Tom anymore. Something doesn't feel right... I mean he is a lawyer and an old family friend... Besides, I swiped it out of Matthew's briefcase."

I handed it to Bryce and watched him silently flip through the pages. He'd stop occasionally and read something, and handed them back to me. "You should get a second opinion on that contract."

The table was uncomfortably quiet. "What?"

Meanwhile, Victor touched April's head. She opened her eyes and screamed. Veronica picked up the crying baby and went into the library with Victor trailing behind, apologizing profusely.

"Maddie," Bryce commented. "Just glancing over it I can see several things that seem off."

"What do you mean off? I read it carefully and it looked pretty good, except for those things I mentioned."

"Well," Bryce put his fork down. "No one owns the mineral rights on this island."

Second, it states you cannot cancel the contract without Tom's signature, and he certainly will not want to cancel the contract."

After we finished dinner Stuart asked to see the contract.

"What the hell, sure." I got angry at Tom all over again.

Stuart pointed at something and handed the papers back to Bryce. He looked up Cellcom on his smartphone while Stuart showed me a statement buried several pages into the document.

"We already told you about the ownership of mineral rights in Catalina." He flipped over two pages, "Here it states you cannot alter any part of the lease on your own, including the rental fee for ten years without forfeiting ownership of your entire property once the tower is completed... and it is non-negotiable."

"What? I guess I didn't understand that part." I knew he was a self-serving jerk, but I thought he was at least honest. He was the one and only person left in the entire world I thought I could trust with my affairs. How could he do this?"

Veronica put her arm around me while the men waited for me to compose myself.

Bryce showed what he found online to Stuart. "I'm afraid there's more Maddie. It states that Matthew Hasenphun who owns Cellcom, is Tom's brother-in-law and Tom is a major investor. That makes him a silent partner."

"Maddie," Stuart said, "Seriously... You should see a lawyer off the island as soon as possible to confirm what we've told you."

I put my head in my hands.

"If you want, I can give you a list of reputable attorneys from the Bar Association."

"Do you know anyone in Serena Beach?" I wiped my eyes, "I wouldn't know how to choose."

"We have a colleague, Jeff Brownlee, who specializes in contract and probate law in Serena Beach." Stuart nodded in agreement.

Dimple jumped in, "Oh yes, Jeff Brownlee. Why didn't I think of him? He has a superb reputation and his office is in the Global Trade Center."

Stuart pulled out his cell. I stopped him and said, "That won't work, there's no coverage on this side of the island."

He replied, "No problem." He pointed to the sky as he walked onto the patio, "It's a satellite phone." After a few minutes, Stuart came back inside. "I called Jeff and gave him a quick rundown of your situation. He's willing to see you first thing tomorrow."

"Is this why Tom wanted to move this along so fast?" I asked.

"If you had signed this," he looked me in the eyes. "and the Cell tower was in place you wouldn't have been able do anything about it."

Bryce put his hand on my shoulder. "If you'll let us fly you over there in the morning, you can get this taken care of... quickly."

Chapter Fifteen

I was dressed and ready to see the attorney Jeff Brownlee when Veronica stopped me at the bottom of the stairs.

"Quick Maddie, I want to show you something before it's gone." She led me into the family room. "Look, it's what I was telling you about."

She pointed to the wall opposite the big mirror. "Do you see it?"

On the wall was a reflection from the big mirror in the shape of an arrow pointing in the corner of the room.

"Weird, I've never noticed that before. It's always so cloudy and gray in the morning and the sun never...hmmmm." I glanced at my watch and noted the time - seven-forty five.

"Well," Veronica said. "I wouldn't have noticed it either only Nicholas and Sarah dragged me in here to see it this morning."

It could just be a weird coincidence, but I was more concerned about my trip to see Mr. Brownlee.

"Bryce and Stuart will be taking me up to the airport in less than an hour. I better eat something."

"I have breakfast ready for you." Veronica responded. "It's not hot, but you'll like it." While we munched on cinnamon rolls, Veronica gushed about how charming Victor was.

"Be careful." I cautioned, "He can be charming, but he tends to exaggerate his accomplishments"

"I get it Maddie. But I think he may have matured a little since you two dated."

"We went out twice, that's all. That's not dating. See? That's what I mean about him."

"I'm older Maddie, so I've had a little more experience at reading people than you."

"Oh," I chewed a mouthful and swallowed, "like Lloyd?"

She looked down at her plate, "That was mean."

I put my arm around her.

"I'm sorry Veronica. I just don't want you to be hurt again by some jerk."

She sulked some more.

"Really. I didn't mean to hurt your feelings. I care for you deeply... and for the children."

She wiped a tear from her cheek. "I know you didn't."

With my copy of the contract and Aunt Helen's will, I was ready to go.

Once at the office of Mr. Brownlee, he confirmed what Bryce told me. "From what I can tell, your finances appear to be in excellent shape. You don't need this deal to keep from going bankrupt." He suggested that I fire Tom as my attorney immediately. "Your name should be the only one on these documents. Since you're over eighteen, there is no longer any need for him to be named. You should have been told this, and there's no reason why you cannot manage your own estate. Getting Tom's name off the documents would deny him any and all access to the inheritance funds and your finances."

He looked at my copy of the will. "This is NOT the complete will. It's only an extract." He called in his assistant, "Please contact the Probate office and have them fax over a copy of this will. The case number is stamped on the last page."

After about twenty minutes, the assistant came in with the fax that must have been fifty pages - it was huge.

"Why don't you get some lunch while I go over this? Could you come back in say, an hour and a half?"

***

When I got back, Mr. Brownlee explained what he had learned, "I know your late aunt's accountant, Phil Endablanque. He's an excellent accountant. He must've realized what Tom was trying to pull, because soon after Ms. DeVine passed, Tom fired him and took over management of the inheritance and financial records. That's why Phil wasn't able to sign checks or pay anything. Tom made up the story about your desperate financial condition. He also had the bills directed to his office and must have piled them away without paying them. On paper it looked like you were getting close to bankruptcy and of course he comes in and saves the day with this cell tower lease scheme."

I sat with my mouth open. "...scheme?"

"Tom lied to you about your inheritance and the cell phone company. I checked and Tom is the one in financial straits, he and Matthew put up their houses to cover costs for the company. If they lost your account they would lose their house and business. Tom was desperate, he planned all this to set himself up and his brother-in-law with this twenty year deal. They'd funnel all your assets through him and you'd never know the difference. You would get a check for the lease, but that is not even a drop of what you've actually invested. You'd be left with nothing in less than a year and his plan was to 'rescue' you from under the fake debt and buy Dove Acres from you, with your own money, I might add, leaving you with nothing."

I shook my head.

"What about my adopted sister Jojo? Is she mentioned anywhere in the will?"

"Who?"

I explained our relationship while he flipped through several pages shaking his head, "She's not listed, but you are given the right to dispense your inheritance anyway you see fit after your eighteenth birthday and after you've fulfilled the terms of the will, which by the way..." He flipped several pages over, "states you must occupy Dove Acres only thirty days. The original document does not state anything about living there six months before you take possession. There is a provision that if you do not accept the terms of the will or commit any criminally punishable act during that time, all inheritance, properties and right would revert to the next of kin - and that would be a Mr. Lloyd Brewster of Purgatory Springs, Missouri."

I looked at Jeff, "Lloyd Brewster was arrested a couple of days ago for assault and breaking and entering on Catalina."

"Really? Then according to the terms of this will he has forfeited his claim to any inheritance. Before Mrs. DeVine... er,"

"It's okay." I interrupted. "You can say died. So you're telling me I only have to remain on the island the rest of the month, then I can give part of the land to Jojo if I choose?"

He nodded, "Plus you can come and go from the island. The document does not say you cannot leave. To occupy means it is your primary residence for that period - like a vacation home... You have your mail forwarded there and you pay the utilities. That's all."

"That's great Mr. Brownlee. I appreciate all your help. What do we do next? Can you take over as executor?"

"Slow down Maddie." He chuckled. "It's good to see you smile, but we'll have to go to court and bring suit against Tom Silverman for fraud and misrepresentation. He could get disbarred for his behavior and there may even be criminal charges against him. Are you ready for that?"

I stood up. "Bryce, Stuart and Dimple Outhouse all think highly of you. I'd be honored if you represented me. I want to pay my debt to those who are owed something, so let's do that first."

"I'll have all the necessary paperwork drawn up. In the meantime I will get a temporary restraining order against Mr.

Silverman to prevent him from doing anything else under the guise of executor."

I felt pretty good after getting some good news for a change.

***

I couldn't put off dealing with the letter I got from the bank any longer so I flew back to the island with Bryce in time for my meeting.

Mr. Woodfin's secretary took me to the same conference room where I'd been the other day only to find Luke's father, Pinkie, Jojo and a man in an Aloha shirt sitting around the table. Mr. Woodfin greeted me with a smile, "Miss Maddie." and showed me to my seat.

Pinkie and Mr. Garrett stared at their folded hands, while Jojo stared at me. "We called this meeting to request that you not erect a cell tower on Dove Acres.

I was shocked, how'd he know? He must have read the confusion on my face.

"I checked out the men you met with here the other day. I know they're from Cellcom and we put two and two together."

"We?"

"Maddie," Pinkie began, "We are part of a citizen's group here that look after our little island. We only want to preserve it for the future."

"I thought," Mr. Garrett Sr. broke in, "it would be better if a small group like us met with you to discuss your plans instead of a mob."

"A mob?"

"Many of the island's citizens are upset by what they've heard my dear." Pinkie jumped in, "it was all we could do to convince them to let us talk to you before they began to picket Dove Acres."

"Picket? Are you serious?" I can't believe this. How in the world could they know? Why would they care since it's on my land, away from view of the beach!"

Mr. Woodfin went on, "We have very strict laws here of what can and cannot be put up on the land. We understand you are a...well, new to the island and probably are not aware of the restrictions we have on building and machinery." The banker was smiling all the time he was talking. My confusion turned to anger. I tried to keep the lid on it while I heard them out. I wished Mr. Brownlee was here.

"I don't want the tower built on our land." Jojo stated. "It's not for you to ruin the ancestral land of the native people who lived and cared for this land before you got here."

The four of them looked at me, waiting for me to respond. I tried to think what Aunt Helen would do? Compromise?

"First of all," I answered, "All I want is what's best for Dove Acres. It's my family's land and my inheritance. I need to keep it going and not let it to fall into disrepair."

This was none of their business. Where am I living? Nazi Germany? "I haven't made a firm decision regarding the cell tower. Yes, I did meet with several gentleman a few days ago but nothing was decided."

"We don't want the tower. Period." Jojo demanded.

Mr. Woodfin glanced at Jojo and turned to me. "We don't feel the tower is in the best interest of the land. We want to see if we can persuade you not to follow through with your plans. Mr. Garrett has briefly shared his thoughts on your ideas of making Dove Acres a bed and breakfast inn.

"And why is your opinion important to me?"

Mr. Woodfin's face reddened, then Pinkie glared at Mr. Woodfin. "Whether or not the B and B is allowed is not the issue right now. This group is concerned about the environmental, cultural and economic impact the cell tower will have on the island."

"You can have a study done, there are several professional groups that provide that service." Mr. Garrett added. "It'll take time, and I understand time is of the essence for you. But it needs to be done appropriately in order for your plans to be completed legally."

"First of all, this is private land, my attorney assured me I'm exempt from several of the laws that govern commercial land. Secondly, I've said over and over, this is my land, you can't tell me what, when, where, or how to conduct my affairs." I took a few deep breaths to calm down. "Please just stay out of my business. I will bring any issues that concern the community to your attention and follow legal channels. Other than that, mind your own business."

Pinkie stood up. "We're trying to help and head off a demonstration on your property. We came because we're your friends."

"You're no friends of mine, as of now. And you..." I looked directly at Mr. Garrett. "I'm very disappointed. The next time we meet Mr. Woodfin, my attorney will be present."

I stormed out of the room, ran down the stairs and headed to the shore. I was betrayed again, and this time by Pinkie of all people. I honestly thought I had friends. Jojo has made her feelings known since that day she came to see me. But the other two, how could they do this to me! No wonder Luke kept saying he didn't deserve my thanks. He was planning this all along. That S.O.B. I must be a lot more naive that I thought. People on the street stopped and stared at me bawling my eyes out. I didn't want Veronica and the kids to see me like this. They've had enough drama to fill a lifetime.

After calming down, I wiped my eyes on my sleeve and walked to my cart.

On the way back to Dove Acres, my cell phone rang. I pulled over onto the dusty shoulder. It was Pinkie. "What do you want, traitor?"

"Maddie, I'm not going to lecture you."

"I should hang up on you right now for turning on me."

"You know, Mr. Garrett and Jojo may have been doing you a favor warning you about how upset everyone was. How would you feel if they knew about a demonstration and didn't tell you."

"Pinkie, I really don't need more excitement right now. Just need some alone time."

I hung up and drove home. Veronica came in from the garden and I threw my arms around her. "How would you and the children like to live here forever? I would love your company and your children are wonderful."

What I really wanted to say was - Please, please stay. You're a terrific cook and if my plans go ahead, I'll need you.

"Wow. Where did all that come from?" Veronica asked. "I said we'd only stay a couple of weeks, and you've been more than generous."

"I won't take no for an answer. You've been my anchor with all my troubles and I love you guys for being here."

"If we do stay, I'll insist on doing the cooking for you."

"It's a deal then. Let's shake on it. If we can stay with you, I will do all the cooking and help with the cleaning until I find another job here on the island or on the mainland." Oh my gosh. I thought I just died and went to heaven. She gave me a warm hug.

"Oh, one thing Maddie, Nicholas starts first grade in the fall. If I don't find another job by then, do you mind if we use your address to register him?"

"No problem. We'll just deal with those things as they come up."

I hope she doesn't find another job yet and I'm not ready to tell her about the letter or the meeting at the bank yet. My head was spinning - maybe I was having a breakdown.

"By the way, Pinkie asked if I could help out at the store. I guess Raylene left unexpectedly, so I'm taking the children with me this afternoon."

"That's great. See, things are looking up already. I'm going to my room and read for a while."

Chapter Sixteen

Very early the next morning after the meeting at the bank, I heard someone pressing my doorbell over and over again. I instantly decided that I wasn't a morning person as I rushed to put on my sweats. Hobbling towards the stairs, I had both feet stuck in the same leg of my pants which I discovered, is one of the disadvantages of sleeping in only your underwear.

Dimple was at the kitchen door, hysterical, "Oh Maddie, there are a bunch of people demonstrating on the road by your gate. I could hear them chanting from my house."

"Demonstrating? Chanting? Please call the Sheriff." I ran out the front door to see what was going on. There was smoke coming from the direction of the road. I could hear sirens approaching, but when I got there the demonstrators had already gone. The fire department put out the grass fire along my fence and took pictures of the damage, which amounted to some graffiti and a few burnt patches on the lawn.

The fire captain said, "I guess no one had a good enough arm to reach your house and the fire didn't do much damage. Your tall fence and gate kept them off your property."

"Thank God for that."

Deputy Lopez stepped up, "We arrested two people leaving the scene." He read from his notes, " Raylene Moffitt and Jojo Ruiz, everyone else got away. There were too many of them for the two of us on the initial call, but we know who most of them are." I looked over his shoulder and saw Jojo and Raylene sitting in the back of the Sheriff's truck.

"Jojo?" I yelled, "Why are you doing this? You're my sister!" She turned her face away. Raylene just scowled at me and yelled, "Bitch!"

I looked at the deputy, "Did they say why they did this?"

"Not really, Ms Ruiz hasn't said a word." The deputy held up a hand to me and spoke a couple words into the microphone attached to the epaulet of his shirt, "Roger that, our ten-twenty is Dove Acres. We'll be ten-fifteen with two in a few minutes."

He looked at me, "Ms Moffitt, on the other hand was jabbering nonstop and I couldn't understand her. We'll run a drug test on both of them back at the station."

Soon the twins ran up and found Dimple with me. With all the deputies milling around, it was difficult to grasp what had just happened. I felt like I was having a nightmare and couldn't wake up, and if I didn't wake up I'd die.

"Miss Van der Wald." A female deputy said, "We need to survey the rest of the property. Could you please come with us." Large yellow letters spelled out SHERIFF on her olive green vest and two men with boxes were waiting for me. "Did they make it into the house?" She asked as we left the burnt areas of the grass by the gate. I shook my head.

One started taking pictures as they accompanied me to be sure nothing else was damaged. Thankfully everything else was okay.

"You shouldn't stay here alone. Come stay with us." Dimple demanded, "Now get your things." Quite frankly I was numb to all of this right now and followed her lead. My overnight case was right where I put it yesterday. I hadn't even unpacked.

"Thanks Dimple, but what about Veronica and the children?"

"Bring them too. I have plenty of room."

Dimple's place was a welcome, hidden fortress, away from the craziness that seemed to be following me.

"No one will know if you are going and coming."

Bryce and Stuart were waiting at Dimple's for her and the twins to return.

"Maybe it would be prudent to hold off on any building or changes to the property until you have documentation that the land is indeed a Tongva burial ground." Bryce suggested. Stuart thought if we pacified the media with a little information here and there they might leave you alone until you make a decision.

"Can't I at least, go ahead and start planning for a bed and breakfast inn."

"You'll need some advice and consultation from people who don't have a stake in this place." Bryce said, "You can't do this alone."

"Tell me about it, I don't have a clue where to start with any of this. I appreciate everyone's willingness to get involved."

The room went silent.

"If you want me to pay you for your help I'd more than happy to pay your hourly fee. Bryce, I need your connections to the media, Stuart I'll need your help with the Indian Council and Dimple, you could be a liaison between me and the island residents."

"Don't worry about money Maddie. Lord knows none of us need any more." She winked at the twins and their friends."

Jimmi added, "We all loved Helen and she cared for us. We were like family, all of us."

"I hope I didn't insult anyone by offering to pay you, but Mr. Brownlee told me you both are the best I could possibly have at public relations and Native American culture."

"That was very good of him. We'll get right on it." Bryce assured me.

Dimple offered to put an editorial in tomorrow's local newspaper, "Perhaps it would be best to wait a day or two before you go into town and when you go, don't go alone. Let one or two of us escort you."

Now I was scared. I wanted to talk to JoJo but that would have to wait since she was in jail.

I felt safe enough to go for a walk along my beach. There were no boats anchored out there and Lloyd was in jail along with Raylene and unfortunately Jojo. I sat on a rock, closed my eyes and let the sun warm my face.

"Hey Maddie." A voice startled me. I looked up, with my hand shading my eyes from the sun. "It's me."

"Luke?" I slid off the rock, "What are you doing here? Do you know what your father is up to? Who the hell does he think he is?"

"Well, I happen to agree with him on this subject."

"Go away."

"Please hear me out, this may be our only chance to talk."

"Why? Are you afraid what will happen when that protest group finds out the son of one of their ringleaders is talking to the enemy?"

I reached for my cell phone. I held it up toward him, "See this? I had to buy a satellite phone because my cell didn't work on this side of the island. This is why a tower might be a good thing for the island," and headed for the path back up the hill.

He ran ahead of me and blocked my way. "You can have me arrested for trespassing and false imprisonment when you get back to the house, but first hear me out."

I had no choice. "You've got two minutes then I'm going to call the Sheriff."

"I knew you were going to have problems with some of the people in Avalon when word got out that you were planning to put up a tower. Pinkie and I felt it would be in your best interest if we worked within the group rather than openly siding with you. There were too many of them against you. Don't get me wrong, I don't believe the tower is in the best interest of the island either, but you have the right to choose for your own property. I'll defend anyone's right of free speech and pursuit of happiness. Anyway, Pinkie and my father were hoping we could defuse their anger by working with them, that's why the formal meeting with Woody to show them you were trying."

He paused, "Some people may have thought your aunt was a kind hearted eccentric. But she was a sharp businesswoman. She always learned all she could before she made a financial decision. That's how she maintained the family fortune and land all these years without her husband. It wasn't through stupidity. Whoever told you she was crazy, stupid or naive is lying. Eccentric doesn't mean stupid."

"Not that it's any of your business, but I inherited a mess that I'm trying to sort out. I was about to tell you what my aunt's so-called attorney was up to, but your little group assumed they knew what I was going to do. I felt ambushed and betrayed at the bank."

"Maddie, do you really want to be the loner on the island, fighting for your own existence. Do you really think people will frequent your inn if there are picketers constantly at the front gate?"

"Luke, if you aren't going to let me talk and hear what I have to say, then you can just get out of my way."

He dropped his hands to his sides, "Pinkie, my father and I really care about you."

I ran past him and up the path, looking back to see if he followed me. When I was alone, I walked crying, back to Dimple's house alone. "Why did I ever open Tom's letter in the first place? My life was going along just fine. I may not have been rich back on the mainland, but I didn't have all these problems."

I found Veronica, sitting on the patio. I composed myself and asked, "Where's Dimple?"

"She's off shopping with her nieces and their guys."

"Mind if I join you? I'm pooped."

With the warm sun and cool breeze, I quickly fell asleep.

What seemed like a few minutes had passed when I heard the sound of children's voices.

"Auntie Maaaa - Deeeeee... Wake up... Auntie Maaa - Deeeee"

I forced one eye open and looked at my watch. "Six p.m.?" I said out loud, "How could it be six p.m. already?" I hate when I fall asleep for so long. Nicholas and Sarah grabbed my arms and pulled me into the house.

"Come on Auntie Maddie, time for thupper." Nicholas explained, as they tugged me towards the dining room.

"You guys slow down, I'm right behind you." When I got to the dining room, I discovered Dimple and Veronica had prepared the most wonderful salmon cakes and asparagus. Nicholas climbed up on his chair while I lifted Sarah up onto the telephone book placed on her chair to make her tall enough to reach her food.

Afterward we sat with Dimple and watched a movie in the den. The house was quiet. Maybe I should get a dog, a Rottweiler or Doberman would do the trick - oh wait, they might eat Nicholas and Sarah. I'll have to think about it.

Chapter Seventeen

I thanked Dimple for letting us stay with her before going back to our house. She wanted us to stay longer but three days was long enough and the excitement was over.

I felt secure now that we were back home and could sleep in our own beds again. But in the middle of the night we were awakened by blaring sirens and flashing lights. Baby April was crying and she was joined by screams of terror from Sarah and Nicholas. Veronica gathered up her children and tried to calm them while I rushed around looking out the windows, at the same time dialing 911.

"We have an intruder," I told the Sheriff's, "please hurry."

"We got it here too, we're on our way."

I hustled Veronica and the children into my room, locked the door and wedged my desk chair under the knob like I'd seen on TV. We huddled together on my bed and grabbed my trusty floor lamp, ready for battle. Anxiously, we watched the door. In my other hand I held the cell phone, waiting for a call from the Sheriff or the security company. At this point, I really didn't care which one. When my phone finally rang, I crawled over the duvet and picked it up. "This is Maddie Van der Wald." I answered in a shaky voice.

"Deputy Torres here. Please stay inside. We've apprehended a trespasser. He was caught on the fence on the Outhouse property line. We're taking him down to the station right now. He's pretty combative, and yelling stuff that doesn't make much sense."

"Thank you so much deputy." I turned to Veronica with her little ones clinging to her nightgown, "They caught him."

"Thank God." She whispered and slumped against the headboard.

"The Sheriff's taking him down to the station right now. If we left the kids with Dimple, would you come with me this morning to see who it is?" She nodded.

"Now, let's all try to go back to sleep." I could tell she would rather have her fingernails pulled out with pliers than go down to the Sheriff's station and risk encountering Lloyd again.

I punched my pillow into a comfortable shape, closed my eyes and easily fell asleep.

***

The next morning was sunny and breezy. I phoned Dimple. She whispered back, "Hi Maddie, is everybody at your house asleep? After your security system woke everyone up at three a.m., the girls and their friends stayed up all night, drinking and talking. What happened? Was it the hole digger?"

"I hope so." I explained that Veronica and I were going down to the Sheriff's station to make an identification, and asked if she would you watch Sarah, April and Nicholas?"

"Oh my, I'd love to, just bring them over."

Dimple greeted us with a finger to her lips. "You have to be very quiet, everyone is still asleep." Nicholas was in his superhero pajamas and Sarah clutched her blanket. "Okay." Veronica handed wide awake April to Dimple. "What a sweet little face." Dimple tickled April's tummy and got a bubbly smile in return. Veronica kissed the two older children and assured them she'd be back soon. "Now listen to Auntie Dimple and do what she says. I love you."

We quietly backed out the door, got in the cart and headed for Avalon.

"Before we find out who this trespasser is, I'd like to talk to Jojo and find out why she is acting so hateful to me."

When we arrived at the station, I was taken to a small room with two windows that looked like telephone booths. I sat down in the visitor's room and waited until the deputy brought Jojo to the counter on the other side of the thick glass window. She sat down with her eyes downcast and her hands in her lap. I picked up the pay phone-looking handset, "Jojo?" She wouldn't pick up the telephone handset on her side. Deputy Torres tapped her on the shoulder and handed it to her.

I said, "How are you Jojo?"

She didn't answer, but looked at the ceiling.

"Luke came to see me today."

She silently glared at me.

"He wouldn't listen to me either."

She looked away again and smiled.

"Jojo, I found out that my aunt's lawyer lied to me." Without looking up, she smiled again. "Please look at me. We're family and I love you."

She glanced up, scowled and stood up. "I am Tongva and proud of it. THEY are my family." She turned to leave. I could hear her say to the deputy as she walked through the door, "I'm done here." My heart was broken. I thought we were kindred spirits. How could she turn on me? What did I ever do to her? I felt numb. Deputy Torres escorted me back to the front office where we told to wait. We waited a bit longer until we heard the steel door of the cell area slam shut. Deputy Torres said, "That'll be Deputy Nguyen bringing the suspect up for identification."

When I turned around to look through the window I couldn't believe what I saw. "Victor Minotti, what the hell are you doing in there?" Victor looked at Deputy Nguyen, "See, I told you I was Victor Minotti, I'm not with Lloyd whatzit? I haven't dug any holes and I sure haven't beat any kids or women... Are you going to let me out of this poor excuse for a jail? I have to get back to Rancho Mirage. My car is there, my golf clubs, My life is there."

I looked at Deputy Torres, "Where are Deputy Lopez and Deputy Murray?"

"They're at a training session in Pomona. We're filling in for them."

"What's he charged with?" Deputy Nguyen flipped back a few pages in his notepad and read, "Criminal trespass, Suspicion of vandalism, Drunk and disorderly, Resisting arrest, Assault on a deputy sheriff, and in general – being a prick. All night long, all he wanted to do was call either you or his mother."

"Victor... your mother? Not your attorney? Really." I sighed "That's sad... I'm not surprised, but I'm very disappointed in you."

He shrugged and looked at the floor. The deputy sat him down and handcuffed him to the chair, then motioned toward the office door, "Let's go up front."

"Oh, there you are." Veronica said nervously when we came through the door. "I get the creeps when I know Lloyd is close by."

From the other room, Victor shouted, "Hey... What about me? How long do I have to stay in here? I want my attorney." The deputy closed the door.

"Do you want to press charges?" He tossed a copy of Victor's booking picture on the desk in front of me and asked, "You know this guy?"

Embarrassed I nodded, "Unfortunately, I do."

"We picked him up at three-thirty this morning trying to jump the fence at Dove Acres. First he claimed he was your boyfriend."

"Oh God." I groaned, collapsing in a chair next to the desk.

Deputy Nguyen continued, "Then he claimed he was staying the night at Dimple Outhouse's place and was going to your place to visit Veronica Christensen when he got hung up on the fence. That little prank set off the alarms, floodlights and triggered an armed response."

I looked up at them, "He's not my boyfriend, Deputy. I don't have a boyfriend.... I mean - I don't have a steady boyfriend. Look Deputy," I explained, "Veronica and I had dinner with Dimple Outhouse and her family. Her nieces brought their friends and Victor, er... Mr. Minotti with them. I don't know what he was doing on my fence in the middle of the night, but I don't want to press charges, I just want him to go away and leave me alone."

"So..." the Deputy said, "You used to date this guy and your friend was married to him for three months?"

"No, she wasn't married to him, she was married to Lloyd Brewster, the alleged hole digger."

"...and you dated him?"

"No, I dated Victor, the guy you caught on my fence."

"So, he's your boyfriend... this Victor Minotti..."

"No! Look, I'll say it again, Victor's not my boyfriend. I haven't gone out with him in almost two years."

"Okay... I got it."

I sighed, and applauded, "Finally. Can I go home now? You caught a different guy, the wrong guy. You already have Lloyd Brewster in custody. He's Veronica's nutjob estranged husband... my dopey third cousin, the suspected hole digger and my friend Veronica is terrified of him."

The deputy confided that they've had a bit of trouble with Lloyd. "He's been harassing one of the female prisoners across the hallway from him, specifically, Raylene Moffitt. It looks like we may have to transport him down to Two Harbors while he awaits trial."

Tom was waiting by the gate at Dove Acres when we got back. I definitely think a big dog might be a great investment.

"Why?" was all he could say.

"What's wrong with you?" I shot back. "Didn't you think I'd find out?"

"I needed help, you were the only one who could help. I may lose everything. All of it because of you."

"Why not ask for help rather than trying to scam me?"

173

Tom gave no response but walked away, then turned, "I meant all I said about how I felt for you. I'll change everything, give me another chance. I'll re-write the contract. I need the tower. I..."

"You expect me to believe anything you say?"

Some part of me felt sorry for him.

"Just let me build the tower."

"Get off my property." That was the kindest thing I could say at this point.

"Don't do this to me," he grabbed both my shoulders. I struggled to get free. The more I struggled the tighter his grasp. Somehow I hit the ground hard, my head just missed a rock. I looked up and saw Bryce was standing over Tom. His fists clenched.

"I've wanted to that since I read the contract. Man that felt good." shaking his right hand. Tom rolled over and pointed at Bryce "You're going to be hit with a huge assault charge buddy."

"It was self defense," Bryce insisted.

Veronica shouted from the car, "Yep, I saw the whole thing, it was self defense all right Bryce."

"Then you turned on Maddie here," Bryce replied while he helped me up. "I also see possible bruising."

"Look, he tore my shirt sleeve."

"...and you tore her shirt." Bryce repeated.

Veronica held her cell phone, "I'll call the Sheriff."

Tom stood up with a handkerchief on his nose. "You'll be sorry. You'll all be sorry you ever messed with me."

"Are you threatening us? You really want more problems added to the assault, fraud, embezzlement and conflict of interest charges?" Bryce was very calm and collected. "I suggest you vacate the premises immediately and do not try to contact Ms. Van der Wald except through Mr. Jeff Brownlee, her attorney of record.

I guess that's how lawyers talk to each other.

Chapter Eighteen

With Lloyd still in jail and Victor now off the island, I realized I had to call Pinkie and apologize for not listening to them at the bank. And as much as I hated to admit it, Luke was right. I can't live in a fortress surrounded by fences and security alarms. What kind of life is that? But there was no way I was going to tell him that – he'd never let me forget it.

"Maddie none of us, Mr. Garrett, Mr. Woodfin or Luke was at that protest in front of your place. You know that don't you? We tried to warn you."

"I feel terrible Pinkie. There's just too much happening too fast. Could you tell Luke I didn't mean to go ballistic when he came to talk to me?"

"I'll try to convince him that you won't try to kill him."

Later that afternoon, Luke called. I was ready for gloating.

"Hey Maddie. I still haven't collected on our flying fish bet."

He didn't say I told you so and most importantly, he didn't mention the cell phone tower.

The next day when he came by to collect on our bet, Nicholas had already run to the front door with his bug can in hand. Sarah toddled after and tugged at Luke's shirt. He gave them each a hug, "Okay, let's see whatcha got." Nicholas pulled the plastic lid up and Luke looked in. "Wow. You got two crickets and what're those?"

Nicholas glanced inside the can, "a thnail and a thlug."

"You really have a knack with kids Luke." He seemed embarrassed because he hadn't noticed that I was watching.

"You look like a million bucks Maddie. Ready to go?" I nodded and gave the kids a hug.

Veronica picked up Sarah, "You guys have a good time. Maybe you'll see some flying fish."

"Hey," I whined, "who's side are you on?" and I grabbed my backpack. "Don't worry, I'll be back tomorrow before lunch."

The sky was sunny and clear when we walked out onto the green pier. "Here we are." Luke pointed down at a little rowboat bobbing gently in the glassy smooth water. "We're spending the weekend in that?"

Luke laughed, "Are you nuts? That's just to get to my boat." He held my hand as I carefully stepped into his dinghy. "The trick" he explained, "is to sit down in the center of the bench. That way the boat won't rock."

I did my wobbly best and held onto the sides of the little boat while Luke got in and untied the line. He sat facing me and rowed out to his beautiful white sloop. I saw the boat's name carved into a gold trimmed, teak placard on the stern, *Spirit of Lisa* and underneath, neatly lettered in navy blue, *San Francisco*. We pulled alongside and Luke reached up on deck to pull out a short wooden ladder which fit into slots and hung over the side. He set my bag on the deck and climbed up first.

"Just stand straight up Maddie and give me your hand."

I stood up and saluted, "Aye, Aye Cap'n sir."

"Now put one foot on the rung of the ladder and I'll pull you up."

He reached down to pull me aboard, when the wake from a passing motor boat, caused our boat to rock side to side. The little dinghy bobbed and rocked like we were in an earthquake. I grabbed for the side railing to steady myself but missed, the sloop rocked away from me and I fell backward into the water. My clothes were soaked and heavy, but I swam to the surface and treaded water until I saw Luke peering down from on deck.

He dove in and popped up next to me, "Are you okay? Want to do that again?"

I spit out a mouthful of salt water and caught my breath, "Ha ha, no thanks. Not today."

"Come on, I'll help you back on board." We swam over to the side of the boat.

"Grab the ladder and I'll help you up."

Lacking Luke's upper body strength, I dangled feebly from the last rung on the ladder until I felt a large hand on my butt pushing me up out of the water and halfway up the ladder.

Once on deck, I collapsed - soaked and exhausted.

Luke brought up the rest of our things from the dinghy.

"I know this probably sounds like a line from a bad movie, but you better go below and get out of those wet things. There are some blankets and clothes you can wrap up in while we dry off your wet stuff."

Shivering, I nodded. He unlocked the cabin door and showed me in.

I was amazed, "Wow, this is like a house down here."

"I like it..." He replied, "I'm going up top while you get dried off. He turned and went back outside, closing the door behind him. I walked to the stateroom in the bow and undressed. Looking around, I found a pair of crew socks folded up on the dresser and a big plaid flannel blanket. After wrapping up in the blanket, I shuffled over to the door. His head appeared at the opening,

"What should I do with my wet clothes?"

"I assume you brought a change of clothes..."

I nodded and pointed to my backpack on the deck behind him. He handed it down to me and took my wet clothes.

"Hey, these are pretty sexy." He held up my expensive lacy lavender bra... "and wow, I didn't imagine..."

"What did you think, that I wore big white granny underwear?" Totally embarrassed, I slammed the cabin door, "Well, where are you going to put my clothes?"

"I'm going to run them up the mast and dry them, of course."

"Don't you dare, Luke Garrett. I'll never forgive you."

"Okay, okay. I was only kidding. I'll wring'em out and lay them out on deck, no one will see them and they'll dry fast."

I pulled out a pink tank top and white shorts out of my backpack and put them on over my other bathing suit when I spotted a photograph of a happy young woman tucked in the frame of the mirror. The edges of the picture were worn but the condition couldn't hide the beautiful face, blonde hair, piercing blue eyes and radiant smile. I wondered who she is? Every morning when he combs his hair and shaves, there she is. I found my floppy hat, opened the door,

"This is a beautiful boat. I love the smell of the wood and the glimmer of all the polished brass when the sun hits it"

"Thanks Maddie, that's why I keep her... She's perfect."

"Is that why you named her *Spirit of Lisa*? And is that a picture of one of your girlfriends on your mirror?" Shit. I wished I hadn't said that.

"What? No... What picture of... That's my mother. Her name was Lisa. My father named the boat after her and its always bad luck to change the name of a boat. When he bought her they had expected to have a big family by now. But it wasn't meant to be. I was the only child so my father gave her to me when I turned eighteen."

"I'm sorry Luke. It was a stupid thing to say. I didn't mean to..."

"You didn't say anything wrong, Maddie. We've dealt with my mom's death and I'm finally ready to move on with my life."

"Do you remember her?"

"Vaguely, I was only eight when she died. My dad told me she loved to be on the ocean with just the sound of the water and the wind." He fought to keep from choking up. "Her ashes are somewhere out here. We had them scattered on the water at her service. I don't remember much of it." Luke slid his arm around my waist and drew me close beside him.

"Anyway, that's the story of the photo. This is nice having you here. Maybe I should lose more bets."

"Aren't you going to change? You're still all wet."

"Yeah, I guess I better."

Luke squeezed past me in the passageway, his lips passing very close to mine. He paused and whispered, "I'm glad you're okay. You had me worried." I kissed his wet lips and whispered back, "Thank you for coming in after me." I kissed him again. Luke put his arms around me in a warm embrace. I felt a tingle race up my spine and back to my toes, my hands found his strong chest, I slid them up around his neck, and kissed him deeply.

Luke opened his eyes, "I guess I better change," and went to the stateroom. I sat in the main cabin wondering if I was doing the right thing.

He opened the door wearing a pair of board shorts and a long sleeved t-shirt.

"I'm going to untie the mooring line so we can get going." I followed him and watched as he went to the wheel and started the engine. The entire boat gave a muted rumble and we started to move. Slowly, we motored down the line of boats, heading toward open water. Once out of the harbor, I sat down beside him and held his arm tightly.

He looked down at my hands around his arm, "What's that for?"

I snuggled next to him, my hair still damp, "Just making sure I don't fall overboard again."

Luke steered the big sloop near Pebbly Beach where we'd be out of traffic and cut the motor. "Have you ever sailed before, Maddie?" he asked while he untied the mainsail.

"Yeah, I've been out on a sailboat before."

He looked at me sideways and said, "No, I mean, have you ever *sailed* a boat before?"

"If you mean, do I know how all those ropes and winch thingies work, the answer is no, but you're going to show me, right?"

"Maybe later," he said, "I'm going forward to raise the sails. Don't touch anything. When I come back, I'll teach you how some of the thingies work."

I watched as he deftly pulled a rope here, adjusted a winch, tying a knot there... he knew just what to do.

The big mainsail crinkled and popped as the breeze started to fill the huge sail. As it did, we picked up speed. I sat close to him, watching how he steered the big boat, reading the wind. Once we picked up speed, I wandered around the deck until I found a place to lay out and work on my tan while the sloop glided across the waves.

I stuck my arm in the air and waved to him before pulling my hat over my face. Luke crawled to where I was, gently lifted my hat.

"Luke! Who's steering the boat?"

He smiled, "I set the autopilot so I could come over and kiss you," and pecked me on the cheek.

I returned his cheek kiss and whispered, "You are so sweet."

He smiled, "We'll be at Two Harbors in about twenty minutes." I rolled over on my back but watching the top of the mast made me dizzy, so I leveled my eyes on the horizon, just in time to see a gust of wind blow my clothes that had been drying on deck, into the ocean.

"Luke!" I screamed, "My clothes."

He swiveled his head around and saw them floating away in our wake.

"You want me to turn around and get them?"

I leaned over the railing and shook my head no as my new, forty dollar underwire bra slipped beneath the waves, while the matching lavender underwear was plucked out of the water by a seagull and taken who knows where. I sighed and sat back down next to Luke, "I'm not going to need them anyway."

He raised his eyebrows, smiled and winked at me.

"I meant, I have extra in my backpack."

Luke's smile disappeared as he went up front to drop the anchor. "I'm going to set the other anchor too. We don't want to drift onto the rocks during the night."

"No, we wouldn't want that." I replied, as if I knew what I was saying. I guess drifting onto rocks would be a bad thing. As soon as Luke made sure everything was secure, he sat down next to me and swung his arm around my shoulder.

***

I woke up in a bunk below deck. Luke was asleep beside me.

"What's the matter?" He groaned.

"How did I get here?" I demanded, "What time is it?"

"Easy... you fell asleep on deck, I didn't want you to turn into a burnt slice of bacon so I carried you down here and laid you in bed. You were hugging my arm so I let you sleep... See? You still have your clothes on."

"And the sun is setting! How can I sleep away a beautiful day?" I sighed.

"Look at the bright side. You didn't get sunburned."

"Luke, it's not funny, I wanted to have a fun day, and I wasted it by falling asleep." He took my face in his hands and looked into my eyes. "Maddie." he spoke my name so nicely. "After the stressful six days you had with everything. You deserved a nap." He held me and caressed my hair. The beat of his heart was calming.

I sat up, "Getting hungry?"

He nodded. I wriggled out of his arms and went down to the galley.

"I put some things in the freezer that we can heat up." I yelled up from below, "I'm sorry it's not very romantic."

When the food was done, I found that he'd set a small table with a tablecloth, candles and soft music on his mp3 player.

"If I knew this was a formal affair, I would have dressed up." I stuck my foot up and wiggled my toes to show him I wasn't wearing shoes.

Being on the side of the island away from the lights of Avalon, the stars were exceptionally bright.

"Look at that Maddie... millions and millions of stars."

"Absolutely breathtaking," I thought back to the night on top of Veronica's car "I feel like I'm floating in outer space."

"It's kind of like looking at all the spirits of everyone on earth," Luke whispered, "Millions and millions of people, and I was fortunate enough to find you glittering brighter than all the others in the darkness."

I looked at his profile, lit only by candlelight and the stars.

After dinner Luke lowered his inflatable boat into the water and started the motor. Carrying his high-powered flashlight, I climbed onto the stern and got in the boat with him. He handed me a lifejacket, "Hang on!" I grabbed the ropes looped along the side of the boat while Luke twisted the throttle, sending the little boat zooming forward. The wind and seawater smacked my face as the bow bounced over the dark waves.

"Shine the light ahead of us and sweep it back and forth slowly... tell me what you see."

Following his directions, I held the light with both hands, "Oh my gosh!" I shouted, "Look, Luke, Look! They really do fly!" Silvery fish were jumping out of the water and flying several feet above the surface, some glided alongside the boat and across its path. One landed in the boat. I screamed while it flopped and wiggling around my feet. Luke slowed the boat and picked up the struggling fish. He held it up and spread it's fins out. "Wow," I shouted, "they look just like wings."

Luke threw the struggling fish back into the ocean.

"I thought it was going to crash into me. Sorry I screamed."

He laughed, "Don't worry, they don't bite, but they stink and they *do* land in boats every so often."

He turned the boat around and slowly motored back toward the *Spirit of Lisa*. I breathed in the sea air and looked up at the night sky with all its stars.

"Luke? What do you think about when you're out here on the water, alone?"

He glanced in my direction, before turning back to the task at hand, "Nothing except how blessed I am to be here and what I'm doing at the moment. Sometimes I wonder if I'm making a difference on the island, helping the people understand the importance of preserving the ecosystem and recycling. We live on this little rock with finite resources and I was hoping to help preserve it for future generations. Sorry...I'm getting on my soapbox." He eased the little boat up to the side and held it steady while I climbed on deck. "... and now I think about us."

While I took off my lifejacket, Luke went below and brought up some sparkling apple juice.

He poured a little into each of our glasses. "Here's to our weekend of starry nights, flying fish and you."

We took a sip. "My turn. Here's to the night and my very own lifeguard." We raised our glasses again.

"I'm beat even after my nap. Do you mind if I turn in?" I put down my glass and headed to the stateroom while Luke straightened the sheets and blankets in the main cabin to settle in for the night. I slipped off my swimsuit and pulled a long t-shirt over my head. I closed my eyes thinking about the day trying not to think of the past week when I heard a soft knock on the stateroom door.

"Yes?" I asked.

"Oh, I guess you're still awake." he said.

"Well, duh."

Luke pushed the door open a bit and stuck his head in, "I've been thinking..."

I pulled the blanket up to my neck, "Luke Garrett, What are you thinking?"

"Jimmi and Jonnie told you my father had to sell the architecture business. He sold the office buildings, client list, equipment... everything. Even after all the legal fees and lawsuits, he ended up with a few million in cash from the sale of the business... and I got a part of the life insurance when my mother died. So, Just in case you're wondering, I'm not hanging around you to snatch some of your inheritance. I don't need it. I was going to tell you someday, but this weekend, I wanted to be honest with you."

I waited for him to say something else but he just looked at me. "Well, I guess I better say goodnight," and went back to the main cabin, closing the door behind him.

So why is he telling me this? I looked at the clock... four-thirty in the morning. It was still dark. Carefully, I cracked open the stateroom door and peered into the main cabin. Luke was fast asleep on the fold-down bunk. I wanted to kiss him but I didn't. Instead, I went back inside, feeling content and fell asleep.

The smell of something cooking and bright sunshine woke me.

"Hey." Luke smiled when I stuck my head through the hatch. He'd made us breakfast of eggs, kippered herring and toast. A few puffy clouds drifted overhead while a couple seagulls swooped low, looking for handouts. I wondered if they'd comeback to steal some more of my clothes.

"After we clean up, we should head back to Avalon."

I put on my bikini top, and a pair of shorts then went on deck to watch as Luke got everything in order and pulled up the anchor. He raised the sail and turned us toward the sea. Moving slowly at first, we picked up speed as the wind filled the sails and the *Spirit of Lisa* was on her way, cutting across the deep blue waves, heading for Avalon. I joined Luke on deck and took a seat next to him.

"I hate for this to end."

"Really?" He replied. "I thought a city dweller like you would be glad to be back on dry land, shopping and eating in restaurants."

"Give me a break, I like to try new things. Do you think I'd be living at Dove Acres if I was afraid of adventure?"

"I know you came on this trip, reluctantly. Y'know, the flying fish bet and all that."

"I'm actually having a wonderful time, and I've gotten to know you much better. In fact, I may be changing the way I feel about you."

He smiled and looked out at the ocean.

The channel current was with us, we made good time. He stopped the boat and dropped the anchor at another cove.

"Now you can have all my attention, Miss Van der Wald."

"Well, you aren't saying much."

"I was just thinking about you and me..."

"What about you and me?"

"I was thinking how happy I feel when we're together."

"Whenever I get close to you, know what I see?" I sat up and put my face close to his.

"Tell me... Mr. Garrett, *what* do you see?"

Luke whispered, "The future."

I didn't respond. What was I supposed to say? I stared into his eyes, and whispered, "I think... I think ... that you... should check the anchor, I think we're moving."

"Oh crap." Luke jumped up and cranked the anchor chain back taut while I busted up laughing,

"What's so funny?"

"I wish I had a video camera. You are so funny when you're dealing with a crisis."

He unwrapped some cinnamon rolls Veronica had packed for us and handed me one.

"Wait, wait..." Luke shushed me just as I was about to take my first bite. "Listen... The Coast Guard is broadcasting an emergency message."

He hurried over to the controls and turned up the volume on his marine radio.

"Attention. Attention. All vessels in the vicinity of Santa Catalina Island. A male prisoner has escaped from the Avalon Sheriff's Station. Suspect is Five-foot Ten wearing blue jeans and vest with a light beard and tattoos on both arms. Last seen in a gray Zodiac inflatable. This person should be considered dangerous. Do not allow this person to board your vessel. Please report any sightings to the Coast Guard on channel nine immediately.... Attention. Att -"

Luke turned down the volume. We looked at each other.

"That sounds like they're talking about Lloyd. What should we do?

He switched the radio to channel nine and called the Coast Guard. "This is Luke Garrett aboard the *Spirit of Lisa* moored at the Palisades - Is this suspect Lloyd Brewster? Over."

The response came back immediately, *"That's 10-4 on that Spirit. Keep us informed."*

"Do you think Lloyd would head back to Dove Acres?" I asked, "How do I get in touch with Veronica?" Luke scanned the area behind us for any sign of my idiot cousin.

"How could he escape from jail?"

I started to get nervous, "That doesn't mean he wouldn't come this way. He's not too bright, so he might be heading for the cove by Dove Acres."

"Oh my God - Veronica and the children. What if he tries to get to them. Luke - we need to get over there."

He pulled up the anchor. I kept a look out behind us while Luke started the motor and headed for the cove below my cliffs.

I've learned that sailboats weren't meant to go very fast, even with a motor.

"Maddie," he asked me as he steered a straight line toward the cove. "What do you think we should do once we get there?"

I hadn't really thought that far ahead, I only know I can't leave Veronica and the children there alone. I don't know, maybe we can keep him from climbing up to the house or something."

The boat was so slow, it seemed like we were moving through pudding. I could see the cove now and up on the hill, the house sat, open and sunny. Below, the little beach and pathway leading up the side of the cliff. I glanced behind us again and saw something coming around the point.

"Luke! Look."

He picked up the binoculars and looked where I was pointing.

"Is that Lloyd?" he asked handing me the binoculars.

I held the big orange plastic binoculars up to my eyes and focused on the point. I wouldn't ever forget that face.

"Yes. What'll we do?"

Luke picked up the radio's mike and called the Coast Guard, giving out location and that we spotted Lloyd.

The gray Zodiac was getting close. I crouched down where he couldn't see me. Luke went below and returned with a speargun.

I whispered, "What's that for?"

Luke loaded and cocked the speargun. "Fishing." he answered. "I might want to catch something slimy. Now stay down so he doesn't see you."

"Please don't do anything stupid. I don't want you to get hurt."

"Really?" He joked, "You care about what happens to me?"

A raspy voice shouted up from the small rubber boat, "Hey, there on the *Spirit of Lisa*. Can I come aboard?" It was Lloyd alright. "I need to uh, uh, I need to make a radio call."

Luke called back over the side, "No - I don't think so. But you can make a call from the Coast Guard boat when they arrive." Luke leveled the speargun at the inflatable boat.

"Hey, what the...?" Lloyd shouted as he revved the motor on the Zodiac and turned around.

I sat up and watched as Luke pulled the trigger. A spear, trailing strong fishing line behind it, went through the right pontoon of Lloyd's boat. With a loud hiss it began to quickly deflate and take on water.

He turned and looked back at us. "Hey, you crazy sombitch, what'd you do that for? Wait a minute - what's she doing there? That Van der Wald bitch, I shoulda known."

His boat was dead in the water and the heavy motor was beginning to weigh heavy on his chances of staying afloat. As it started to sink. Lloyd moved to the side that was still floating. Luke tied the line to a cleat. The sound of big engines made us look to the sky. We saw a Coast Guard helicopter in the distance. Luke reached under the cushion of his seat and produced a strange looking gun.

"What's that?"

Pointing it skyward, Luke replied "a flare gun. I'm signaling the Coast Guard helicopter," and pulled the trigger. My eyes followed the smoky trail into the morning sky and watched as a bright greenish orange flash appeared overhead. The flare arced over and landed in the water nearby and continued to give off a big colorful plume of smoke. The Coast Guard boat appeared and sped directly toward us, while we waved madly on deck. A couple hundred feet above us, the helicopter continued to hover. When the Coast Guard boat pulled along side, the captain asked through a bullhorn, "Where is this guy?"

I leaned over the side and saw nothing but the spot where the line from Luke's speargun disappeared into the dark water. The deflated boat had apparently been dragged under by the weight of the motor and sank. Worse yet there was no Lloyd. I looked over the opposite side and yelled, "He must have drowned." Luke pointed down at the spot where Lloyd's Zodiac had been. Luke checked around the boat to make sure Lloyd didn't climb aboard when we weren't watching. "What makes you think he drowned?"

"He's from the Midwest." I yelled over the noise of the helicopter, feeling a bit sad for the jerk, "He probably didn't know how to swim." I leaned down and looked over the side to see if I could see him. Suddenly Lloyd popped up, grabbed my arm, and jerked me into the water.

I screamed, "Luke! Help!" just before I went in. Lloyd pushed my head under like he was trying to climb on top of me. I elbowed him in the crotch and pushed him away with my legs. After I got a few feet away I headed for the surface and yelled again. Luke grabbed both my arms and pulled me back onboard the Spirit of Lisa.

The helicopter hovered lower and dropped a diver into the water just as the Coast Guard boat came around to our side. They scooped up a thrashing, gasping Lloyd with a fishnet, hauled him aboard and handcuffed him. Luke cut the speargun line so the Coast Guard could hook up what was left of the Zodiac to their boat.

By the time the Coast Guard and Sheriff's deputies finished questioning us it was after noon. They brought their Scuba divers back up and headed back to port.

I called Veronica and carefully told her what had happened. She was apprehensive but calm. Finally, I could relax with Luke for the voyage back to Avalon harbor.

Chapter Nineteen

When we got back to Dove Acres all I wanted to do was take a shower and get the smell of seawater out of my hair. After I put on some dry clothes I went back downstairs with a towel wrapped on my head. Feeling a lot less stinky I joined Luke and Veronica out on the patio.

"It's almost time for supper." Veronica asked. We both shook our heads. "Let me throw something together for us. Stay here and relax."

I would have offered to help but I knew better than to get in the way of someone who really knew how to cook. In a few moments, she brought us some roast beef sandwiches on sourdough bread. My mouth was watering.

Luke filled our glasses with lemonade and offered, "Alright, a toast... Here's to us, and to the flying fish."

"And to my expensive underwear," I added with a laugh. "Wherever they may be."

Veronica held her glass high, "Here's to dreams."

I took a sip and looked at my two new friends, "Since I've been here, I've finally grown to like island life."

I detected a smile forming across Luke's lips.

"Luke, with your creative and technical talents, we could restore my aunt's house and turn it into an eco-friendly bed and breakfast inn that would complement the area."

He put down his glass and took my hand.

"I'm embarrassed to say this, but after I told you how I felt about building on Dove Acres, I started to think of what I would do if I had inherited the property and...you know what?" He hesitated for a moment, swallowed hard and said, "This is really too weird, but I came to the same conclusion - a eco-friendly bed and breakfast inn."

I couldn't help but throw my arms around his neck and give him a quick kiss.

Veronica commented, "Your boat trip was kind of a bust, wasn't it?"

I shrugged and glanced over at Luke as he took a bite of his sandwich.

He dabbed his mouth with a napkin, "Maybe but we'll try it again."

It was probably too soon after all the craziness.

"What do you say Maddie? Are you up for that?"

I hesitated answering him right then. We've all been through a lot and I didn't know if I was ready try another weekend together yet. Instead, I changed the subject and asked Veronica how she was feeling about the whole thing with Lloyd.

"I'm relieved for my children but I feel very weird. Part of me is happy and wants to jump up and down, but another part feels scared." Veronica looked at both of us, "Does that make any sense? Are you sure he's gone?"

I could hear in her voice that she wasn't convinced that it was okay to feel safe yet.

Luke put his sandwich down, "The Coast Guard and the Sheriffs handcuffed him after I sank his rubber boat."

I tried to comfort her by adding, "He didn't get on our boat and there was nowhere else for him to go except down."

"Maybe I'm being hypersensitive about the whole thing. Veronica confessed, "You were there and you know what happened. I'm just not sure."

Veronica asked Luke to help us clear the table and put the dishes in the dishwasher. After I loaded his arms with dirty dishes and pointed him in the direction of the kitchen, he said, "I really like you Maddie. You aren't the spoiled little princess I thought you when I first met you."

"Spoiled little princess?" I wasn't sure if that was a compliment, but I took it as one anyway. "Thanks - I guess."

We helped Veronica by scrubbing a few pots.

"This sounds funny, but could you just imagine us doing dishes with kids asleep upstairs?" he asked, "Pretty corny, huh?"

He tossed me a towel to dry my hands.

"Why don't you spend the night up here?"

His eyes popped wide, "You want me to stay here with you?"

"Ha ha. Very funny. I mean, we have several guest rooms and you can use one instead of driving back down to your boat."

Veronica reminded him, "You'd get a home cooked breakfast in the morning, not just some toaster pastry and bad coffee."

"Hey," he protested, "I make pretty good coffee."

"Uh huh." Veronica answered. "Anyway, this would be a taste of what a bed and breakfast inn up here would be like, and you can be the guinea pig. And don't worry about oversleeping in the morning. If the aroma of bacon, good fresh coffee doesn't wake you up, I'm sure the kids will."

Luke woke to the sound of giggles and little feet running up and down the hall. Nicholas and Sarah ran by, "Hi Luke - Hi Luke."

"Nicholas, Sarah. Stop running." Veronica called to them from the bottom of the stairs.

While she fed the children I took Luke into the library.

"Just wait here, she'll call us when it's ready. I've learned she doesn't like anyone in the kitchen with her while she's feeding the kids. I think it's her special time with them."

We plopped in the two leather armchairs that flanked the fireplace. "So, how'd you sleep?"

He yawned, "Great. I thought I miss the motion of my boat." He seemed to stare at the base of the wall next to the fireplace.

"Did you ever notice how the sun reflects off the mirror and makes that arrow shape on the wall?"

"Veronica and I noticed that the other day. Weird, huh."

He walked over to the wall and ran his hand along the edge of the fireplace and molding.

"There's something off here." He ran his fingers along a seam in the paneling and turned to look at the big mirror. Shielding his eyes from the sun he could see in the reflection, the arrow pointed at the seam. "Y'know Maddie, something's been bugging me about this room for years. I felt odd, off balance since your Aunt Helen's New Year's Eve party, but I couldn't figure out why. Would it bother you if I check out what's going on with this panel?"

"I guess, if you don't mess it up. You'll be able to put it all back won't you? This is an important room, especially when it becomes an inn."

He got a pry bar from the garage and carefully pulled up the base molding by the floor, then he lifted out the section of paneling. The wall was concrete behind the panel. In the center was a strange door that looked like some kind of leak stained it with rust marks. The arrow reflections now showed on the door with a weird indentation embedded in a circular disk in the center of it.

"I've seen something shaped like that before."

"And look." Luke said. "Where the wall meets the floor, there are a couple of slots."

We sat back in the leather chairs and tried to figure out what we found. Luke's hand rested on the table beside the chair. He picked up one of the shells we found in the cave.

"Hey Maddie, I have an idea." He stood and inserted one of the shells into the slot. As he pushed it farther in we heard a click. We looked at each other. He held up the second one between his fingers... "Should we try this one?"

I nodded and he slid it into the second slot with another click. When he did that, the odd shaped indentation receded farther into the door leaving a deep depression.

Luke stood and found my brooch on top of the mantle. "Check this out." He held the brooch next to the indentation in the door."

"I can't believe this! It's the same shape as my aunt's pin."

"Do you think I should...?" he held the brooch over the recess as if to insert it.

"It's worth a lot of money Luke. What if it gets stuck?"

"But Maddie, don't you want to know what will happen?"

I closed my eyes and cringed, "Okay, do it."

Luke carefully placed the brooch in the indentation. Nothing.

"Well at least a giant boulder didn't come rolling down a ramp at us!" He pressed on the brooch and the circular area popped toward us about a half an inch. Luke pushed on it, nothing happened. He tried to turn the circular disk. It moved about ninety degrees and the door swung open.

All I could say was, "Whoa!"

The door was a safe. That's why I could never find it. I had the key all the time. It was the brooch!

Inside the bone dry safe we discovered a locked steel box, a stack of old documents and five worn manila envelopes. The envelopes contained a whole bunch of old gold and silver coins in individual cardboard holders.

"Wow." Luke said, "My father's cousin collects coins. I'm no expert, but I can tell you that you may have a fortune in rare coins. You should get these appraised on the mainland. My father can hook you up with a reputable appraiser."

The stack of documents included a few stock certificates for some of the most well know companies in the world. I carefully leafed through them, "I better have Mr. Brownlee look at these. There was no mention of stocks or coins in my aunt's will."

"Maybe it was her husband's stuff or even from before they bought Dove Acres."

"It had to have been my Uncle George' because he bought that pin for my aunt."

Luke picked up the green steel box and shook it gently. "I wonder what's in here?"

I took the box from him. "Don't shake it. There might be something fragile in there." I sat back in one of the chairs and tried to remember where I saw a small key. "Wait here Luke, I have an idea." I ran up to my room and grabbed the box with the envelopes I brought over with me.

"What's that?" he asked.

I turned all the envelopes upside down until a small key fell out, but it was too big and didn't fit the lock. I sighed, "How'd you know something was back there?"

"This room always felt weird to me." Luke said, "Like something was off, then I noticed this side of the wall came forward much farther that the left side and the molding in the floor didn't match the other side of the fireplace. I thought for a beautifully built house like this, it was out of place."

The phone beside my chair rang and scared us both. Jonnie called to say the protesters were back on the road outside my gate along with television crews with satellite dishes.

"It's mostly Indians yelling that you want to desecrate their sacred burial grounds.

I corrected her, "Not Indians, Jonnie - Native American people."

"Whatever. They claim you are trying to erect a cell tower on their burial grounds and don't want anything built on it until it's been documented."

"Thanks Jonnie, but they're way behind the curve here. I've already decided not to do the cell tower deal."

"You and I know that, but they are still demonstrating and making a lot of noise. We can hear it from here at Aunt Dimple's house."

Dimple was already knocking on the door. I rushed to let her in.

"The Calvary has arrived, Maddie dear." Her arms were loaded with packages of food. "I know you have Veronica here, but I've brought enough provisions for a lengthy siege."

Dimple began to spread her food out on the big kitchen table when Luke walked in.

"What's the occasion, Dimple?"

Without looking up, Dimple continued unwrapping dishes and setting out plates and plastic cups, "We're preparing for a siege from the protesters and media."

"Maybe..." Luke offered, "Maybe we ought to go out and talk to them."

"I'll go only if they aren't going to throw any more fire bombs at us." I answered.

Luke reminded me that Jojo and Raylene were the ones who threw the bombs and they were still in jail.

"I haven't noticed any new holes since Lloyd was arrested, so I guess he was the one digging the place up."

Dimple stopped unpacking food and said, "Maybe you should try talking to them and clear the air."

"Only if Luke comes with me." I hoped the Sheriff's deputies were there in case of trouble. We walked down the road to the gate where Luke pointed out the local Tongva chief.

"What do I call him?"

"Chief Roundstone is his title but his name is Harvey... Best call him Chief Roundstone."

I walked up to the gate and called, "Chief Roundstone?" They began to chant.

"I'm Madeline Van der Wald, owner of Dove Acres."

Someone shouted, "Hey Luke. What are you doing on the enemy's side of the fence?" They began chanting louder. We noticed that the reporters were enjoying the drama. Luke held both his arms up high. "Please let Ms. Van der Wald speak." The chanting continued. I climbed up on the gate, "Please listen to me."

I swung my legs over the gate and sat facing them. The sheriff's deputies moved forward. I glanced back over my shoulder, there was Dimple and the twins, along with Veronica and the children watching from back near the house.

Some of the demonstrators looked to see what I saw and calmed down.

"Listen everybody, I am NOT going to erect a cell phone tower. That is final. You have my word."

Somebody in the crowd booed me. "We don't trust your word." I looked to see who said that. The group parted so someone could come to the front. It was Jojo.

"I don't trust you."

I looked at her. Her arms were crossed like an American Indian princess in an old movie.

"A lot has changed Jojo, I really need to talk to you."

She looked back at the chief for advice.

He replied "It is not for us to interfere with family matters."

"I'm not trying to discourage you from your Tongva heritage, Jojo. I just want to talk."

The Chief motioned for her to approach me.

I looked at him, "This is personal."

Jojo replied, "Only if the Chief comes with me."

I nodded. The three of us and Luke walked back to the house and onto the deck.

"Jojo," I began. "First let me tell you the lawyer I had was a crook and tried to trick me into the Cell tower so he could take over the property."

"I'm listening." Jojo replied.

"I also learned that he was hiding things from me in the will." I looked at her but she was fiddling with that little key on the chain around her neck. Suddenly I had an idea.

"Just a minute Jojo, I'll be right back." I ran into the library and brought the Green steel box out to the patio.

"What's this?" the Chief asked.

"Jojo, I have to ask you a question... does that key around your neck go to your diary?"

"What does that key have to do with sacred burial grounds?" The Chief seemed irritated.

"No, I don't know what it's for. Your mother said it would bring me good fortune. I guess it's sort of a stupid good luck charm. I don't even know why I still wear it."

She pulled it over head and tossed it on the table.

"You want it? You can have it. You already have everything else."

"We just found this box in a wall safe behind a hidden panel in the library." I picked up the key, held my breath and inserted it in the lock on the front of the steel box. It fit perfectly.

I turned the key and heard a click. The box opened.

Chapter Twenty

I peered inside then turned the box around so everyone else could see. In the box were two bones tied with a braided cord, a small piece of broken pottery, a handwoven cloth bag tied with twine, and some papers, rolled and tied with a cord that looked like it was made from hair.

"What is all this?" Chief Roundstone asked, picking up the bones and the bag.

I unrolled the letter and found it was actually three pieces of parchment. I read aloud.

"Dear Josephine,

If you are reading this letter then you have found the secret to Dove Acres. From northwest of the stable, to the property line lies an ancient Tongva burial ground."

Jojo jumped out of her chair. "I knew it. I just knew it was true."

"Wait a minute. There's more." I read on.

"This portion of Dove Acres belongs to you, Josephine. My grandfather, Herman DeVine met a Tongva woman and gave birth to your grandmother. She was a disgrace to both the Tongva and to the white people because she was a half-breed. Your great grandmother moved to a reservation and put your grandmother up for adoption. The items contained herein were left behind at Dove Acres. I have no knowledge of their significance or what they are but they were very important to her."

I spent years and a great amount of money to help find her descendants. You Josephine, are the only remaining descendent.

With all our love and regrets,
George Devine.
Encl: legal deed to burial ground

Survey of burial ground"

"Wow." Luke whispered.

The Chief held the items and closed his eyes and hummed softly. When he opened them, he looked at Jojo "This piece of broken pottery is a reminder that your birth name in Tongva was Clay Basket. You must keep these things for they tell much about you. I will contact the Shaman. He can interpret the other items for you."

"My - er, our family must've known this day would come for her to give you this key." I explained, "Jojo, I guess this means you weren't forgotten." After I rolled the parchment and returned it to the box, I handed the key and the box to her.

"Here Josephine, I hope we can be sisters again."

"Don't ever call me Josephine. Jojo will do just fine." She hugged me and whispered, "I'm sorry for the mean things I said to you."

The Chief announced, "This is good. I'll tell the people to go and leave Dove Acres in peace."

"I know what I'm going to do," Jojo added, "I'm going to donate my portion of Dove Acres to the tribe so it can be kept sacred as it should be."

"One more thing." I ran back to the Library and came back with two of the envelopes full of coins. "Take these and have them appraised, I'm sure they must be worth a lot." She gave me a big hug and left with the Chief.

I went back inside to find everyone else had been eavesdropping by the French doors.

"That was certainly... amazing... unbelievable." Veronica said, "I'm happy to see you and Jojo put your differences behind you."

Dimple, sounding a bit disappointed announced, "Well I guess the siege is a no go. Does anyone want to take all this stuff back home?"

Luke and I went with her and said goodbye to Bryce and Stuart..

"We'll be back." Bryce commented, "We just have some business to take care of in Palm Springs."

Stuart reminded me, "Luke could be very helpful on your project... his father is a licensed architect, but remember, Luke's very big on the environment."

"The last time the subject came up," I admitted, "We didn't exactly see eye to eye."

"Maybe you can have a talk with him Bryce. We've talked but there's much more to discuss."

"Keep in mind Maddie, he's learned a lot from his father about architecture."

"We'll be ready to obtain the necessary capital as soon as you give the word."

Bryce gave me a peck on the cheek before he left.

I scooped up Sarah and followed Veronica into the living room.

"What about you and Victor, I mean after he got out of jail. Did you guys hit it off?"

"The weirdest thing happened Maddie... He talked a lot about you... I think he's still obsessed with you."

"So I told him to forget about me and my kids." Veronica confided. "He's not over you."

"I'm so over him - in fact I was never into him but now I'm scared I'll have a stalker."

Veronica took my hands, "Madeline Van der Wald, nothing scares you. "

"I think I've fallen for Luke. This is happening too fast."

"I knew that from the day I met you. You need to be straight with him. Better to have a good architect you can work with than a jilted lover."

The phone rang again. "When will it ever quiet down around here?" I complained. "I thought we had this quiet place to build a B&B."

It was Dimple. "Oh, Madeline. I just wanted to tell you Pinkie called and told me that jackass, no offense to your immediate family, got loose from the deputies again while they were putting him on a boat to Serena Beach. He made a big enough ruckus in town to get everyone chasing after him. I heard a few of the men chased him on foot to the Casino and cornered him for the deputies."

"Oh crap." I responded.

"What? Maddie, what's up?" Veronica asked.

"Nothing, everything is okay."

Dimple went on, "Pinkie said they hogtied him and carried him onto the boat. Everyone in town watched until they were out of sight."

A few days later I saw Javier walking toward the house with another person.

"*Buenos Dias, Señorita Maddie.*" Javier called, his face lit up with pride. "This is my oldest son, Carlos."

I stepped down from the patio and shook his hand.

"I pay to bring him, his wife Teresa and little baby Elenita to United States. I can afford it now."

I could tell he was proud to introduce me to his son.

"We fill all those holes okay?" Javier said, pointing off into the distance, "Unless you want to plant something there."

I thought how simple, yet complicated their lives are.

"Carlos, do you speak English?"

Javier looked at his son and pushed him forward.

"Sure, I just finished my studies at the University of San Gregorio in Mexico City."

I was amazed that he had only a trace of an accent.

"What did you study?"

"English, Horticultural science and landscape design."

Javier added, "I get too old, so he help me here to make Dove Acres pretty. But you don't worry... I will pay him."

"Carlos," I said, "I'd like to see what ideas you have for the grounds. And don't worry Javier, I'll pay Carlos."

"Fine *Señorita* Maddie." Carlos said. He looked to his father for approval and continued, "I'll make a design for you to see."

"When Carlos mother get her passport, I bring her and my other *niños* also."

My heart felt full of joy for Javier. I know how much this meant to him and how many years he had worked for this day.

I drove the old Mustang down to the Post Office to get the wad of mail jammed into my post office box. Everyone was talking about the newly discovered Tongva burial grounds and the crazy homeless guy who got arrested and sent to the mainland. I shook my head and turned my attention back to the mail. Most of it was junk addressed to my late aunt Helen but one letter jumped out at me. I read the return address again. It was from Jeff Brownlee, and it was on fancy paper with engraved printing. Carefully, I tore the end off the envelope and pulled out the contents.

"Dear Ms. Madeline Van der Wald,

In light of recent events involving felony crimes committed by and outstanding arrest warrants in several states, previously undisclosed by Lloyd Brewster, alternate heir to the estate of Helen DeVine. As a result of these circumstances, Mr. Brewster has forfeited all rights as well as any and all future claims to all or any part of the Helen DeVine estate, her possessions or monies.

As legally appointed executor of her will, I hereby exercise the option of canceling the thirty day residency requirement for Madeline Van der Wald and transfer ownership of all material possessions and monies to Ms. Van der Wald effective as of the date of this letter.

Sincerely, Jeff Brownlee, esq."
I slid down the wall and sat on the floor. Sweet.

About the Author

Will Zeilinger was born in Omaha Nebraska but spent five years of his youth in Turkey. That experience opened his eyes to travel and with his wife, Janet, they've had wonderful adventures together.

He was a bit late to the writing game, working most of his adult life in advertising and marketing as a graphic designer and illustrator. Will received his degree from California State University, Long Beach. Will's solo novels include: *The Final Checkpoint, Something's Cooking at Dove Acres* and, *The Naked Groom*. He's co-authored *Slivers of Glass, Strange Markings, Desert Ice, and Slick Deal* with wife Janet Elizabeth Lynn. Will's short story *Under the House*, is in the anthology, *Haunted Tales: Stories from Beyond the Grave (UK)*. He's also featured in *Murder U.S.A.* and *Chicken Soup for the Soul: Dreams and the Unexplainable.*

Will lives a few miles from the beach in Southern California and has served on the board of directors at Sisters in Crime, Los Angeles. He currently serves on the board of California Writers Club of Long Beach.

Made in the USA
Coppell, TX
12 December 2021